Sara's Fire

Tales of the Dragonguard

Anna Rose

Published by Sumaire Press, 2018.

SARA'S FIRE

First edition. May 21, 2018.

Copyright © 2018 Anna Rose.

ISBN: 978-1393979593

Written by Anna Rose.

Also by Anna Rose

Tales of the Dragonguard
Aya's Dragon
Sara's Fire

The Sumaire Web
Siofra
Fiach Fola
Droch Fola

Watch for more at www.sumaire.com.

AUTHOR'S NOTE:

I promised you another story about dragons, and here it is. I'm sure you've already noticed that this story is longer than the first.

Several thousand words longer.

Sometimes, more words are needed to get the story across to the reader. This was one of those instances.

Enjoy *all the words!*

AYA'S DRAGON was quite fun to write. It was something very different from my original genre, which is paranormal fiction. It made me think differently about how things would work with the characters I created. I already tend to micromanage my characters, and with this story, that was not any different. I used to think that was a bad thing, but then, I can't be the only person who has been mentally dragged out of a story by some plot aspect that made absolutely no sense.

Yes, even in a universe not based on our own reality. I am weird that way.

With **SARA'S FIRE**, the main character's natal culture is the opposite of Aya's, so that will naturally affect Sara's life and her worldview. Aya had to fight to get what she wanted in her life. Sara's situation is a much different situation.

I wrote things this way to reflect the way the real world is today. If you think about it, culture is different not just between countries, but even between individual cities and States. What is normal and acceptable in one is anathema in another. This is also reflected in local idioms, so where in AYA'S DRAGON, Our Heroine referred to her mother as "mama," in SARA'S FIRE, the common idiom for the female parent is "mum."

Such is a society in general, which can be a shame, depending upon circumstances. I don't believe that societies should be homogeneous, but I do believe they should be more tolerant of difference within their own communities. It is my hope that such a thing will be a part of our near future in the world and not just a pipe dream.

But I digress.

Never fear, gentle readers. There will be more dragons in your future, and I have not forgotten about Aya, Sentinel, Drannar, and Clarion. While they are not the focus of this story, they are still present, to one degree or another.

The series is currently planned to consist of four stories, each with at least 26,000 words. The next story, on which I've already been working, is called **KAL'S HEART**.

Before you ask, yes, there will be a softcover omnibus edition offered when the series is complete, but be aware that the purchase price will reflect its greater size. The eventual *e-book* omnibus version will also have a higher price. It *will,* after all, be four stories all collected into one e-book.

Thank you again, my dear beta readers, for all your help. PickleNick, Mister Moose, James, Jill, and NJ – you rock!

A particularly grateful nod goes out to the wonderful Daniel, Keeper of Kitchens and Fine Beer. Your thoughtful suggestions have helped to make some of my writing go along much more...er...smoothly.

What beer pairs best with Fire-breathing dragons? Inquiring minds want to know. My current favorite is Wreck Alley, a dark and tasty Imperial Stout.

If you're old enough to drink legally, look it up for more information – and then try some.

Special thanks go out to Ekaterina, Cynthia, Annisa, Nancy, and all the beautiful ladies at 80k.

Now, on to what you really want...
DRAGONS!

1

"Sara! What are you doing, girl? Stop fiddling with your hair and go help your sister!" Patience was gone from the speaker's tone at this point, and there was no more opportunity for procrastination.

"Sorry, Mum," Sara called back over her shoulder and sighed. She twisted her long, curly mass of locks into a plait, then folding the resulting braid in half and binding it all together with a tight band close to her skull at the back of her head. She sat back and turned her head a little to the side, examining the result.

Here and there, untamed hair ends poked out throughout the otherwise tidy braid, but they were contained enough to keep them from being an annoyance. She gave a quick nod and smiled at her work that was reflected in the mirror, pleased with the results. "Just finished. I need it up off the back of my neck. It gets in the way if I let it hang there."

"Really, young lady, I don't know why you spend so much time on it. If it's such a bother, cut it short," her mother said, not for the first time, nor even the tenth. "Your sister has been far more sensible about things that way!"

Once again, the advice was ignored as though it was a passing breeze. Comparing one sister to the other was never a wise thing for Sara's mother to do. As well as her daughters got along, there still existed a small amount of tension between the two that was just an example of the normal sibling rivalry that crosses the myriad iterations of sibling relationships that exist in the vast multiverse. Sara's normal response was to drag her feet when she was compared to her industrious and driven sibling.

"I know, Mum, but I like to wear it long when I'm not working," she said, stepping out the solid mahogany door and out into the dawn's weak light. Another blistering day in the shop, helping her older sister forge an order of horseshoes and mending some items.

"And short hair makes my face look odd," she muttered under her breath as she closed the bottom half of the door behind her. She kept her voice low to keep her mother from hearing her, but still had the satisfaction of *knowing* she had said something aloud.

"I'll bring a hot dinner down to you both at noon, Sara," her mother called after her through the top half of the Dutch door. "No need to come up to the house, I know you'll be busy working."

"Thank you, Mum," Sara looked over her shoulder and called back with a broad smile on her face, now feeling upbeat. A hot dinner sounded so much better than a slab of stale bread topped with a smear of butter or preserves, which was their normal dinner fare. It did not help that it was their habit to devour the scant meal between hammer blows at the hot forge. It was a reason to be happy. "I'll let Pharis know!"

With the top edge of the sun still only just peeking over the horizon, little more than a few spears of golden light reaching into the sky, the morning air remained a bit chilly. Never one to enjoy the cold, Sara moved quickly toward the warmth of the smithy, which had been built about twenty meters from the house, where there would be less chance of random sparks igniting the thatch that covered the roof. Judging from the sounds coming from inside the smithy, Pharis, Sara's older sister, was already hard at work within.

Always one to complete as many orders as possible in the day, she would have started the farrier's work order as soon as she was done breaking her fast. On a normal day, that meant having a portion of whatever was left from the previous night's meal accompanied by a heavy mug of steaming black tea that had been sweetened with a drop of honey and lightened with a bit of cream that had been provided by one of the two cows the family possessed.

Sara stopped just outside the heavy door and looked inside the glowing interior of the smithy. She noted that her sister had pulled her own short length of hair back at the nape of her neck, twisted it into a stubby braid, ragged and singed hair ends sticking out all higgledy-piggledy from its edges, and bound it tightly in a wide dark ribbon of indeterminate color. The leather cap her mother continued to insist she wear to protect it hung, long-ignored, on a far wall, where it had begun to collect random cobwebs.

Even at this early hour, beads of sweat already glistened on Pharis' broad, unlined forehead, her hands and cheeks filthy from her labors. Sara's sister had never been one to ease into her workday. She dove into her work each day like the early bird hunting for its first worm to break its fast.

Sara was not surprised by what she saw, as her sister was less concerned with appearances, and more intent upon getting to her forge and to working as early as she could each morning. Pharis had never been one to cling to the dictates of appearance and fashion, instead preferring to wear clothing sensible for whatever occasion she faced.

The same was true of her diet when left to her own devices. Sometimes, when she was in a particular hurry, Pharis would grab up whatever was close to hand and munch on it as she took the pebbled path to the smithy.

Their mother tried to keep nourishing foods close by for those mornings but was sometimes irritated when Pharis would grab part of a loaf of the previous day's bread accompanied by a thick smear of butter, rather than the dried fruit and nut bread or savory meat pasty her mother would leave on a plate, under a napkin for her dutiful daughter. It was always a bone of contention between the two.

Pharis had explained many times to her mother that she did not feel that she needed anything so special and that she would do just fine with the simple fare she substituted. Predictably, those reasoned arguments fell on her mother's selectively deaf ears.

To Isleni's way of thinking, a piece of unaccompanied bread and butter did not and could not provide the kind of energy a person needed to stay active for an entire morning. Having been raised by a mother and also a grandmother who tended to be plump, and being near to that herself, it was second nature for Isleni to be heavy-handed with food. It was fortunate, then, that neither of her daughters had slow metabolisms, and that their work kept them active enough to burn off what they consumed during the day.

Sara, never a morning person, did not have the kind of internal drive to dash out the door and off to the forge before the sun had so much as brought its blush to the horizon, so her mother often had to encourage Sara to start her day. Isleni did not begrudge the extra effort on her part, as she had always been a doting mother to both of her children. She knew that once up and about, they would keep busy until they were done for the day.

A strong cup of black tea laced with an oozing honey-dipperful of dark buckwheat honey and a dollop of fresh, thick cream was an excellent tool for energizing tired bodies and brains. Sara's favorite tea was one that when left in the teapot to steep long enough, became almost black in color. Isleni could not drink the stuff, as it made her feel jumpy and a bit nervous, but Sara appeared to thrive on it. Indeed, the girl took a lidded large pewter tankard full to the brim with tea every morning.

She took a long, careful sip of hot tea as she crossed the threshold into the warm smithy, swallowing down the last mouthful of coddled eggs her mother had made for the morning's breakfast. Her sister looked up, saw Sara, and gave a welcoming smile. She gestured toward the back of the room.

"Oh, there you are, Sara! I thought you were sleeping the day away! Could you please bring me more blocks from the supply room? I'm nearly through the first batch," Pharis asked her sister as Sara approached. She effortlessly threw a heavy leather apron at Sara, which the girl just as effortlessly fielded and put on.

You did not carry about heavy pieces of metal and wield a blacksmith's hammer without developing significant strength. That was a given. Both young women's considerable strength had come as a surprise to the occasional stranger who was foolish enough to think of women being "the weaker sex." The smart ones left the young women alone at the first rejection. The more stubborn individuals left in a bit more pain. Neither young woman allowed pestersome people to dally for long in their vicinity.

Sara ignored her sister's jibe about sleeping in. No one in the Intelo household slept past first cock's crow. She recalled a few times where she had awakened the slumbering rooster while going to collect the night's eggs, reaching beneath snoozing hens to pilfer the body-warmed ovals laid during the night. Her habit was to wake when he first welcomed the morning with his raucous greeting, and then sit up in bed with a single candle burning, either reading or doing a bit of darning. With Pharis almost dashing about the room in her preparations for her day, it was easier to stay out of the way.

There was always too much to do and never enough time to get it all done in the course of the day. If there were some way to create more time, Sara would have leaped at the opportunity, but reality being what it was, she would need to allow it to pass in its tediously monotonous manner.

"Mum said she would bring dinner down to us today, Pharis," Sara said as she brought over a wheelbarrow full of iron ingots. "I've no idea what she has in mind, though."

"Wonderful! Whatever it is, I'm sure it will be delicious. We can get more done if we don't have to eat up at the house," Pharis enthused,

7

never taking her eyes from the curved metal she was carefully shaping on the edge of the forge. Leave it to the girl to be enthusiastic about swinging a hammer over a hot forge. "You can toss the bread in the box to the hens, I suppose. They'll enjoy the treat."

Doing as she was bid, Sara reflected that she did not possess the kind of enthusiasm for work her sister did but knew it needed to be done, nonetheless. It kept the roof over their heads and food in their bellies, and not having to work for someone else as some sort of servant was a preferable living situation.

"How many sets of shoes did Garland request?" Sara asked. "You tore shreds out of him the last time he ordered only a few."

"He said he wanted five full sets this time, one small, two medium and two large," Pharis replied, gesturing at a grubby scrap of paper pinned to the wall. "I made sure to write it all down as he said it to me. I even made him sign it to confirm it."

Her sister nodded her approval of her sister's ingenuity.

"This is the last shoe from a set Onari ordered from me yesterday. I don't know why he insists on shoeing that bitty pony of his, but if it's what he wants, who am I to gainsay him?"

"You mean that tiny horse with the hooves that are smaller than the palm of my hand?"

"The very same."

"I imagine the shoes last a long time. That animal barely weighs anything! I thought he already had a set made a long time ago."

"He does, but these are different. This time, he ordered them made of silver!"

"Silver? Whyever for?"

"Who knows why the man wants what he wants, but if he is willing to pay for them to be made, who am I to question his motives? He clearly loves the animal. He takes it everywhere with him, after all."

"I suppose so," Sara replied. "It just seems so odd."

"They're probably twice the thickness of an oyster shell, so they're not very heavy at all. Maybe as heavy as one of Mum's wrist bangles," Pharis explained further. "They're for show, more than anything else."

"I suppose they'd have to be, but won't they get scuffed up a bit when he puts them on?"

"Not my problem," Pharis told her with a sigh of resignation. "My part of the arrangement ends with his paying me for my work and handing them over to him."

"Well, whatever happens, it will get him even more notice than he receives already," Sara noted with a one-sided smile.

Everyone in a twenty-mile radius knew the story. One did not easily forget an encounter with the unusual companions.

Onari was rarely seen without the little horse, which he had raised from shortly after its birth when the beast's dam had rejected it. Raised indoors and fed on rich goat's milk, the small horse had thrived and rewarded its human with the kind of love Sara had before only seen bestowed by dogs upon their masters.

"We all have our odd moments, sister. Leave the man to his," Pharis advised with a soft smile. "His oddness harms no one, after all."

"As you say, sister," Sara agreed.

"So, twenty shoes for Garland," Pharis murmured as she glanced at the indicated order from its place on the wall. She mopped the sweat from her brow. "I can't imagine the man will use them all in a month's time. Too many of his customers prefer him to reuse their old ones if they haven't been lost and can be salvaged."

"It's best to be thrifty, Pharis," Sara reminded her sister. "I'd certainly try to reuse a shoe if I was able."

"It's what most of us would do, Sara. Garland is most often like a peddler who will do his best to get as much money as he can from a customer before they come to their senses and walk away."

"His son told me that he has decided to stock up against a rainy day, and thinks he will get a better deal if he orders more at a time. As long as he pays, why worry about it?"

"Because he will try to drag out that payment for as long as I'll allow it, Sara. Anyhow, how did you get Solom to give you that information?"

"I gave him half the sweetcake Mum made me for dessert the other day. He gets quite talkative when he is stuffing his face," Sara explained. "The boy's a slave to his stomach, although I still cannot understand why he is not fat because of it!"

"He burns it all off apprenticing for his father. If he wasn't kept as busy as he is, he would be huskier. Anyhow, he is sweet on you, Sara," Pharis opined, hammering another horseshoe into shape. She ignored her sister's snort of amusement. "He always has been."

"He is not my type, Pharis," Sara replied. "If I ever do choose to marry, I want a husband from among the Dragonguard. You know that."

It was an old joke between them. Sara had decided long ago that if she were ever to marry, it would be to one of the elusive Dragonguard, and as her chances of even meeting one were almost non-existent, she would remain single. Isleni was not well pleased with her younger daughter's intransigence but knew better than to argue the point with her.

Now old enough to marry, Sara had rejected any number of suitors in recent months, including a few who would have been able to give her a very comfortable life indeed. There was no societal expectation of her marrying, so there was no pressure from that quarter.

"Sara, the chances of your meeting a Dragonguard are little to none," Pharis laughed. "You're a smart girl and not at all unattractive, but have you ever seen a dragon and his rider land long enough to court someone, much less have a conversation? Consider Solom. He is intelligent, thoughtful, and has a good sense of humor."

"You consider him, Pharis. I'm just not interested," Sara replied with a snort of laughter. "And why would I want Garland as my father-in-law?"

"Then you should not have shared that sweetcake with him, foolish girl. He is going to think it means something."

"It only means that I couldn't eat the entire thing by myself, Pharis. Mum always makes them too big!"

"Yes, but Solom doesn't know that."

"He should. Mum's made them for him at least a few times since he was a little boy."

Sara laughed and continued to sweep the smithy, supplying coke for the forge as it was needed. The sisters gossiped, joked, and laughed until Isleni arrived with a covered tray, an indulgent smile on her broad face. It made her happy to hear her daughters laughing as they worked.

Pharis had nearly completed Garland's order for horseshoes, so Sara was sorting through their other jobs in order of importance. The stack of jobs was almost an inch tall, arranged in order of importance, all piled up in an ornate but shallow metal basket Sara had created when she was only just learning her craft.

"Venison stew for dinner! Kanil Baros traded me a fresh foreleg in exchange for some embroidery I did on short notice for him," their mother announced from the doorway, carrying a towel-covered covered tray in both hands. "Come help me with this, one of you."

Pharis put her hammer down and took the tray from her mother, bestowing a kiss on the older woman's broad forehead as she then turned to put the tray down on a nearby table. Sara felt her stomach beginning to rumble in anticipation of the feast to come.

It was no secret that Isleni did amazing things with even limited ingredients available, but when it came to game, no one could cook it as she did. Isleni was near-plump for a reason. Not only was she an excellent cook, but she also made sure to taste what she created during the cooking process. She had long ago drilled into her daughters the idea that one should never trust anything served by a skinny cook.

There was no question but that the girls would happily devour what she had brought them and then look around for more. It was something that brought their mother happiness and pleasure at this example of their robust appetite.

Lifting the light cloth cover from the tray's contents, the famished young women were greeted by the welcome sight of a tureen filled to the top with hot, thick, aromatic venison stew, root vegetables emerging here and there from the steaming gravy-like broth, warm golden brown bread rolls, fresh salted butter, and baked, sugared pears for dessert. It was an unexpected feast, and Pharis commented as much to her mother.

"There is nothing wrong with indulging yourself every once in a great while, Pharis," Isleni replied. "The opportunity presented itself, and I took it. Enjoy it while it's here and still hot."

Pharis snorted and would have said something else, but Sara's stomach growled loudly with hunger. Pharis' followed suit not a moment thereafter, and it was her mother's turn to snort in good humor.

Knowing their mother as they did, they knew there would be leftovers already set aside for them for their supper. Dinner was usually the most substantial meal of their day. When the end of the workday came, none of them was energetic enough to assay a heavy meal.

"Aren't you going to join us, Mum?" Pharis asked politely. Isleni demurred with a wave of her hand, which did not surprise either girl. Both knew that Isleni preferred to eat at the kitchen table, rather than in the sweltering air of the smithy.

"Oh, I sampled plenty of it while it was cooking, love. I have that embroidery to finish, and might as well do it while there is still sun out to do it without needing a candle. I'll see you two when you're done for the day!"

Sara watched as her mother walked up the path, back to the house. She chuckled and smiled as she watched Isleni take careful aim at a small rock on the pathway and kick it away, the hard leather of her shoe making a loud, satisfying *thock!* at the impact. Once again, it was good to see the return of joy to Isleni's stride, her heavy cloud of grief finally giving way to blue skies and sunlight.

"Why in the world would he need something embroidered," she asked aloud. "I did not think Baros was into that sort of thing."

"You can ask her about it at supper, Sara. Sit down and eat dinner while it's still hot," Pharis replied, serving out the stew. "There's still a lot of work to do after we're done here."

Sara obediently sat and began to eat, the first taste of the delicious stew wiping all other cares from her mind. If food could heal, Isleni's stew could work magical cures.

"Oh, I forgot to tell you earlier. Randic was waiting for me when I got to the forge this morning," Pharis said, a spoonful of stew poised at her lips. "Asked to be remembered to you."

"I can't recall the last time I saw the man," Sara replied. "I'm not normally down here when he comes by."

Pharis laughed, covering her mouth to hide the food that remained in her mouth. It was the type of polite behavior that should come naturally but rarely does.

"I can probably count on the fingers of one hand the number of times you've been down here early enough to see Randic," she snorted. "He brought some interesting news."

"The man is full of gossip, Pharis. What tall tale did he spin this time?" Not all of Randic's stories were absolute truth, as he seemed to enjoy gilding the lily, as it were, but they were almost always worth a listen.

"I don't believe this one was a tall tale, Sara. He told me there appears to be a flamehound den just outside of Wolthrip."

Randic was an itinerant tinker who came to the forge every month or so to buy the odds and ends he required to conduct business. When he arrived, he also shared whatever bits of news and information he had picked up during his absence. A flamehound was big news, as the creatures were very rare. The tiny village of Wolthrip was a few leagues to the north.

"A flamehound? Really? How did he hear about it?" This was interesting enough to make Sara pause. She had seen some drawings of the beasts in the village and had always wanted to see one in the flesh.

"The local constable arrested a hunter who was intent on poaching the poor thing," Pharis explained further. "They're taking things seriously and have been cracking down hard on poachers. The man is actually facing a prison sentence over it."

"That's good," Sara opined. "They're beautiful animals, and there is no good reason to hunt them. They're not even edible!"

The flamehounds under discussion were large creatures that resembled giant bats, being about the size of a small pony. They possessed membranous wings in proportion to their size that allowed them to fly long distances and muscular hind limbs with clawed toes that could double as hands when necessary.

Folktales had it that flamehounds were peaceful creatures, only living up to their name when harassed. Sara had always harbored a secret hope that she might one day encounter one of the creatures and perhaps befriend it.

For a time, the leather of their wings had been a popular thing to use for clothing, especially rain capes, until almost the entire local population had been decimated by hunting. There was some hope the species would rebound, but no one was sure if the current population would be able to accomplish that feat.

"There are lots of rabbits and squirrels in that area, so it will likely stay in the area until the pickings get thin," Sara said. "Dorner used to tell anyone who would listen about the flamehound that kept his melon field clear of rabbits. Hunters got that one while they were still legal to hunt."

"I remember," Pharis said, wiping up the remains of her stew with a torn-off bit of roll and then popped the dripping morsel into her mouth. She wiped her mouth with her napkin and stood. "It was a shame. Maybe we'll see more of them someday. For now, it's time to get back to work!"

"I hope so," Sara replied, and returned to work, the strange conversation soon fading from her mind. Right now, there was some gold wire that needed her attention far more than the amusing stories of an old man.

For the remainder of the day, Pharis worked on a few small jobs, and Sara continued working on a set of delicate silver ear bobs that a local woman had requested for her daughter's Naming Ceremony. Local custom had it that parents waited a full month before the formal bestowal of a name upon their newborns, something that had its roots in the days long ago, when infant mortality was an unhappy fact of life.

With intense care, Sara engraved the tiny curved surfaces with flowers and leaves, as the mother had requested. She finished them off with the locking screw backs that would prevent the child from taking them off by accident.

It was this kind of clever work that kept people coming back to the warmth of the Intelo forge. They knew a good thing when they saw it.

Little Anarina might not appreciate them now, but with maturity, she might develop an appreciation for the work that had gone into their creation.

Sara fingered the shining Naming Ceremony ear bobs that decorated her own ears. They had long ago been removed to the high point of her ears to make room for the other ear bobs she wore, each a remembrance of some special event in her life.

2

The Intelo family was not well off, but they were financially comfortable. It was fortunate, perhaps, that Pharis had stubbornly followed her late father down to the smithy each day, almost from the moment she had been old enough to walk. It had not taken long for her mother, laughing at her husband's consternation, to tell him that he should appreciate his unexpected apprentice and benefit from any assistance she could render, while she was willing.

Pharis had begun by 'helping out' in whatever way her father needed at the time, dragging a single ingot of pig iron over to where he stood, and fishing finished cooled pieces of metal out of the quenching bucket. Amazed by his daughter's tenacity, Farél set her to more challenging tasks and stood by while she accomplished them and went looking for more challenges.

As Pharis grew older and stronger and he realized that he would not have any sons to take over from him, Farél had started teaching his oldest daughter his craft in earnest. He had hoped that one day he would be showing a son how to swing a hammer and create everything from heavy equipment to delicate filigree, but such a thing was not to be.

As luck would have it, his eldest daughter had shown a keen interest, and Farél, no fool he, had embraced that enthusiasm and smelted and hammered it carefully into the healthy and capable young woman who now did the lion's share of keeping the family afloat. His pride in her accomplishments knew no bounds, and his regret at not having a son to carry on his trade faded entirely.

Sara was nowhere near as interested in smithing as her sister, but recognized it for the necessity it was and so did not complain about her work, although she would have much preferred doing something else with her life. She had learned to pick good prospects out of the pig iron stores, to swing a hammer, wield tongs, when to quench, and was a dab hand at delicate work. A reluctant apprentice she might be, but Sara knew her job as well.

The sisters had significant muscle development in their chests and arms, the result of the work they performed, but unless those parts of their anatomy were bare to the world, they were quickly concealed with feminine frippery.

Farél Intelo would have happily continued teaching his eldest daughter, but for the tragic accident two years earlier, that had first crippled his soul and then taken his life. The path of a blacksmith was no walk in the park, with each day at the forge holding the possibility of severe injury or death.

By some quirk of fate or whim of the gods, Pharis had not yet gone down to the smithy on the morning it happened. Isleni had gotten into a disagreement with her eldest daughter about something insignificant and had been arguing with Pharis, delaying her early morning removal to the smithy.

Both women were strong-willed and unlikely to bend in the face of disagreement, the daughter reflecting her mother. Only when the shuddering rumble of an explosion shocked their argument into suspension did they go, nay, run, to the now ruined smithy.

Pharis had found her father's broken body under a pile of rubble, his legs crushed and severely burned by some of the great stones that had once kept the forge's fire caged and as tame as ever a fire could be. Only the enormous strength she had developed over many years of working alongside her father had allowed Pharis to lever the stones from his legs and get him the medical help he so desperately required.

With skill honed from years of practice, the healer had healed Farél's burns. Unfortunately, she had been unable to repair the damage anywhere near well enough to allow Farél to walk again. The determination was that he would experience things for the remainder of his life from the seat of a wheeled chair, unless he preferred to drag himself along the ground to get from one place to another.

The chair Pharis created for her father had been a work of art conceived between her wheeled invalid's chair that one commonly encountered, the iron wheels of this conveyance were made large enough that Farél could wheel himself around. His upper arm strength was still significant, from all his years swinging a hammer, so he could quickly propel himself along, providing the ground beneath the wheels was unobstructed and reasonably smooth.

Pharis had done everything she could think of to keep her father interested in life, but it seemed that his will to live was shattered along with his leg bones, and no amount of cajoling on his eldest daughter's part could break him free of the malaise that encompassed him. For a time, it seemed he was doing better, but it did not take long until his wife and daughters realized that Farél, beloved husband, and devoted father, had given up. Without the ability to support his family, he felt useless, and so Farél slowly wasted away.

The morning he slipped into the Void, his wife and daughters had been at his side, murmuring words of love and of sorrow. His passing was peaceful, as he had slipped into a deep sleep some days before, and when his time came, he was gone between one breath and the next.

As part of that ritual that has existed perhaps since Time began, those who knew and respected Farél Intelo and his family had come by for his funeral services. Some took the time to clean grief-neglected rooms and tend to hungry livestock, others thoughtfully leaving fresh-prepared meals and cakes behind as they returned to their own busy lives.

There had been those unscrupulous folk, who always exist in the multiverse, who tried to take advantage of the new widow and her daughters, but they had been disabused of the notion that these were delicate flowers, ripe for the picking. Most took the hint and left when confronted, as many such characters are cowards at heart.

Only one nominal gentleman had required more physical disabusement of that notion. He had tried to force his unwanted affections upon Pharis, despite her polite refusals. He had not been a small man, and it had become very clear that he was accustomed to getting his own way using physical intimidation.

His dire threats, and then his agonized screams and pleas had fallen on deaf ears. The mallet's blunt head had perhaps been a little too close to the fire before Pharis picked it up. The stench of cooked flesh permeated the small room with Pharis' first blow.

The man perhaps regained the full use of his index fingers, but only if he had managed to find an exceptionally skilled healer to set the bones and repair the damage they had sustained from the hammer Pharis had wielded against them.

Sara was not as physically imposing as her sister was, although she was still quite strong. She had been the one to hold the interloper's hands in place while Pharis swung her hammer down upon his extended fingers. His screams as he ran away, his ruined hands held tight to his chest, were chased away by the sisters' chiming laughter.

The village constable came for a visit the next day. After a short chat with the two young women, he had nodded his understanding, laughed at the man's foolishness, and then gone on his way, one of Isleni's hot meat pasties wrapped up in brown paper for later consumption.

Isleni had been inconsolable for weeks after her husband's passing. Theirs had been a love match, which, while not unusual, was rare in the strength of their bond with one another. As it often happens when one is widowed, suitors appeared on their doorstep who would have happily taken Isleni's hand in marriage and genuinely cared for her.

Isleni let them all know in no uncertain terms that her heart had been given to only one man and that she would abide in the knowledge that they would be together again in the Afterlife. Until that time, she would continue to care for her daughters until they married or went on the next adventure in their lives. Once that time came, Isleni may have already made plans for her future, but whatever those ideas might be, she did not share them with her children.

3

"I sent the boy to the farrier's to tell him he can pick up the shoes tomorrow morning, first thing," Pharis said to her sister as they were cleaning up for supper. "I should have sent him earlier, but I wasn't sure I'd have them all finished by sundown today."

"The boy" was a local lad called Manu, whom they had taken in only a few weeks earlier after his parents had perished of the plague. He was scrawny as a half-stuffed scarecrow after surviving his own bout of the plague, but he was good-hearted and useful around the place, and his stomach was not so large they could not fill it when necessary.

"Why not have Manu just take the shoes to the farrier and pick up the payment at the same time?" Sara asked reasonably. "Kill two birds with one stone and all that."

"Sara, the boy can barely pick up his dinner plate, much less a full load of horseshoes. Also, I'd rather get payment up front. Garland delayed paying me for my work last time, and I have no desire to repeat that experience. It is not as though I would have problems selling the shoes elsewhere," Pharis explained. "I let him do that to me once. Never again."

Farél had taught his eldest daughter about more than just swinging a hammer and tending a forge. He had also shown her how to bargain and bill. She had been a quick study at those lessons, making him proud.

Manu returned just as Isleni was putting the iron pot of stew in the middle of the kitchen table. After washing his hands in the kitchen bucket without being bidden to do so, Manu sat down at his place, waiting for further instructions, hands clasped in his lap.

"So, boy, what did Garland say when you told him and brought up payment?" Pharis inquired. "Did he put up much of a fuss?"

"He wondered why I had not brought them with me, Miss," he replied. "He thought I should have brought at least some. So he could check their quality, he said."

"Check their quality?" Pharis exploded, her eyes flashing with sudden rage. "What is that supposed to mean? I'm the only decent blacksmith within six leagues of his home, and he is too cheap to travel that far for supplies."

"I'm sorry Miss," Manu said contritely. "Did I do something wrong?"

"You? Wrong? Heavens no, Manu, you did just fine!" Pharis replied her fury cooling as quickly as it had flared. "Garland is the one in the wrong, here, but don't you ever tell him I said that!"

"Oh no, Miss, I'd never tell him such a thing!" The boy still looked worried. "You have my word on that."

Sara patted Manu on the shoulder reassuringly, squeezing it in a friendly way. She felt some of the tension go out of his shoulders at the contact.

"You're fine, Manu. Pharis will deal with Garland when he comes by tomorrow morning. He is coming by tomorrow morning, isn't he?"

"Yes, Miss, he is, but he was very angry and said he thought he should get a discount for having to pick up the horseshoes," Manu had an expression of faint outrage on his face when he said this.

"Did he really say that to you, Manu?" Pharis wanted to know.

"Well, he did not say it to *me*. More like under his breath, but he did say it!" His outraged expression remained.

Interesting. Garland seemed not to realize that while the boy was not the most substantial mallet in the bucket, he was an almost perfect parrot of everything he heard. That could prove useful, Sara thought, if people considered Manu insignificant enough to ignore.

"Did you let on that you heard what he said, Manu," Pharis wanted to know. "You know we've spoken about this before."

"Oh no, Miss. I thought that since he said it so quiet-like, I wasn't to say anything about it!"

"That was good of you, Manu," Sara said. "You keep such things to yourself, at least until you are alone with Mum, me, or Sara."

"My dad and mum told me the same thing, Miss," Manu assured them. "I listened real hard, and then told them what I'd been told! Da'd beat me some hard if I didn't recall proper."

"Properly, Manu. You're a smart boy," Pharis corrected the youth absently. "He should not have beaten you, Manu."

"S'alright, Miss Pharis," Manu stoutly replied around his last spoonful of hot stew. "Da said it was the best way to teach me my lessons."

"Beating doesn't teach anyone anything except that some people like to hurt others, child. No one is going to be beating you here, Manu," Pharis said. "You have my promise on that."

"I won't be beating you, either," Isleni told him, and cut him an extra-thick slice of the pie she was now serving out. Translucent, deliciously spiced and sliced tart green apples spilled out from the edges of the wedge of pie, almost glowing with lots of thick, sweet juice. Isleni plopped a spoonful of whipped cream on top of the steaming treat, looked at the skinny child for a long moment, and then added a second spoonful.

The boy stared at his plate greedily but made no move to eat. Was it the result of good manners, or trauma? Sara both wanted and did not want to know the answer, but refrained from asking the child.

"Go ahead, Manu, dig in while it's still hot. Please eat your dessert," Isleni told him. "Don't let that whipped cream melt. Eat it all up!"

Released from his extreme self-restraint, with a cry of joy and disregarding the pie's heat, the boy dug in with his spoon, stuffing his mouth with the tasty treat. Whipped cream dotted the end of his nose, which he rubbed off with a clean index finger that he then licked clean.

The three women sat and stared at Manu as he devoured the hot pastry, oblivious to the impression he had made upon them. Not even appearing to realize what she was doing, Pharis passed over her pie to the boy, as did Sara. Manu happily applied himself to this added windfall. Sara noted to herself that the child, being so very skinny, probably had a hollow leg to fill up with food.

"When you're done with that, Manu, would you mind clearing the table," Isleni asked. The boy nodded affirmation while continuing to eat. "I have some other things to finish up before bed."

"Did you finish that embroidery today, Mum," Pharis wanted to know. "What did he want you to do for him?"

"It's about half done. I will finish it up tomorrow or the day after that. His daughter is being married in a fortnight, and her grandmother insists that the veil's edge is embroidered with blue posies for good luck," Isleni replied. "She has always been a superstitious woman."

"Audra is being married? I never even knew she had a suitor," Pharis exclaimed.

"Nor did I, but it appears we were in the dark," Isleni said.

"You have your own superstitions, Mum," Sara chided her mother, nibbling on the last piece of thickly buttered bread. The salty bread and butter tasted wonderful after a long day in the forge-heated smithy. "Don't try to pretend that you don't."

Isleni turned beet red and made a feeble noise of protest, but Sara put up a hand in dismissal, shaking her head.

"When you spill the salt, you always pick up a pinch of it and toss it over your shoulder, and you insist that leaving a hat on top of a bed is bad luck," she continued. "I never heard the end of it the last time I tossed mine across the room, and it landed on my pillow. When an owl hoots outside the window, you panic for the next week, terrified that one of us is going to pass away."

"My mother taught me those things, daughter of mine," Isleni replied tartly. "Don't you presume to instruct me, child."

Sara raised an eyebrow at her mother but said no more on the subject. The embroidery request had led to this beautiful meal, and she internally admitted to herself that nitpicking was counterproductive to digestion.

After supper, the women settled down to domestic duties. Isleni spun their freshly dyed and dried wool into both fine thread and bulky yarn, while the sisters industriously dusted and tidied their small, whitewashed bedroom before returning to the cottage's main room to join their mother and Manu. A colorful pile of already-spun yarn rested in a muslin-lined woven reed basket at her feet, each rabbit or sheep's wool skein weighing somewhere between two and a half to three ounces each.

"Pharis, could you please bring in the red wool from the drying racks? Put gloves on when you do, this time. No sense in staining your fingers again," Isleni said, breaking the companionable silence that had suffused the room. Sara giggled at the memory of her sister's green-stained fingertips. Pharis glowered at her sister in silent reply, her expression deadly. "Sara, you get the light blue rabbit wool, please. It was nearly dry when I checked on it this afternoon. The dark blue sheep's wool needs to keep drying at least until after sunup tomorrow."

"What are you going to do with all this wool, Mum," Sara asked her mother, already pulling on her set of waxed leather gloves designed for the task. "You normally don't keep this much of it on hand, especially already dyed."

"I've arranged to trade with Olima the seamstress for some silk thread she has and that I need. It's expensive stuff, but I have no choice, and yarn and thread are much cheaper than copper and silver when we already have the sheep and rabbits to provide the fiber we need."

"What do you need silk thread for, Mum?"

"Never you mind that, Sara," Isleni said curtly, gently testing the strength of the fingering-weight lavender rabbit wool yarn she had just spun. "Just do as I ask and be quick about it. I'll be up late tonight, getting it finished."

Sara looked at her sister, who shrugged and then led the way out to the wool drying racks that hung from the beams of the lambing sheds. The beams were festooned with a painstakingly arranged rainbow of colored fibers created from everything from rabbit and sheep's wool to cottonwool.

"I had not realized that Mum had been so busy with all of this," Pharis murmured, her eyes wide at all the colors revealed in the flickering yellow light of the oil lamp she held. "Where is she going to store it all? I don't think there's any open space left in the house for most of this!"

"We may have to rework one of the lambing sheds, then," Sara suggested. "This one would be satisfactory since it's not being used right now. Let's see about getting some good lumber for shelves, and we'll get it set up as soon as possible. I really don't want hampers full of stored yarn up against our bedroom walls again."

Pharis grunted agreement and went to gather up her assigned armful of wool, Sara followed suit with hers a moment later. The slightly bitter smell of fresh dye tickled her nose, and she had to turn her head to keep from sneezing all over the soft blue rabbit wool. Mum would have had good reason to have a fit over something like that.

Before they began cleaning, Pharis opened the bedroom window to let in the refreshing night air and to chase out any negative spirits that might be lurking in the room. This was something their mother had taught them from the time they were small children, and it had become a habit once they were old enough to do it for themselves.

Pharis began to sing an old nursery song about the plague as she worked, and Sara automatically joined in, giving a soft accompaniment to the melody. As she sang, Sara wondered why so many nursery songs were so dreadful. Very few consisted of happy subjects.

"Cheerful thoughts there, sister," Sara noted as the song came to an end. "What brought about that song? *The Pretty Pony* would have been far more uplifting, I think."

"I hadn't thought about it, really," Pharis replied. "I wasn't trying to be depressing. Truly I wasn't. It just sort of popped into my head, and I started singing."

Sara made a sour face and gave a final swipe of her dust rag on the wall shelf.

"I'll keep the happy thoughts, thank you, Pharis. I'll leave you to the dark ones."

"I'll try to have happier thoughts, Sara," Pharis teased her younger sister, throwing the fresh-plumped pillow she held onto the top of the bed. "I would not want to disturb your delicate soul."

"See that you do!"

4

"Well, Manu's certainly a different kind of smart, Pharis," Sara said to her sister as they bedded down for the night in the feather bed they shared, washed up, damp hair neatly combed and braided, and both thoroughly tired out from their long day's work. "Who would have guessed such a thing?"

"Smart is smart, and while he might not be bright, he is smart enough to tell us what he heard Garland say," Pharis opined. "I think we give him far less credit than he deserves."

"That trick of his would be dangerous in the wrong hands you know, Pharis. Can you imagine him being sent on some sort of spying adventure?"

"Don't I know it, so at least he is with us and not someone who would take advantage of him. I often wonder if his parents knew of his gift for such things."

"I doubt we'll ever have an answer to that question, Pharis. I would think that if it were known by others, the village would have had a much easier time finding him a home after his parents died. You do remember how quiet and standoffish he was after he arrived here, do you not?"

"Mum had to work just to get him to put two words together, yes," Pharis allowed. "I think his life was rough even while his parents were still alive."

"The life of an itinerant worker is never easy, from what I have seen. He and his family followed the crops, going where they could find work for as long as possible, before moving on to the next farm. I don't know how he could ever have had more than even a rudimentary education."

The sisters had been indifferent students, but they had still excelled at their schoolwork. The local school was excellent, unlike some they had overheard being discussed. The relative wealth of the community had helped in being able to secure a suitable teacher and provide appropriate materials for the children's education.

The girls had had some basic schooling while they were younger, but nothing more extensive in scope. Reading, writing, and mathematics had been the principal fields of study for youngsters who would have to work for a living. Neither read for the mere pleasure of it, but then, neither had been exposed to the concept of doing so.

"I'm glad that Papa had a settled business. I would hate to live that kind of life. Blacksmithing might be hard work, but I can do it in one place," said Pharis. "I don't have to go out to find my customers. They come to me when they need my services."

"They come to you if they want the job done right the first time," Sara interjected. "Did you not get one of Tonifee's former customers just the other day?"

Tonifee Eran was a blacksmith who did business in the village, and while his services were inexpensive, those who chose to engage his services soon learned they got what they paid for. Most of his business came from travelers who did not know any better.

"Yes. A newcomer to the area called Heren. His plow blade needed mending and Tonifee was not equal to the task."

Heren, an expatriate Monisian who immigrated for political reasons, purchased a farm belonging to a widow who was unable to work the fields and wanted to sell it off and move in with one of her sons in another village. He had given her a reasonable price for it, including the equipment and remaining livestock. Some of that equipment, however, had long been in need of repair. Such was the often the case when making that kind of a deal.

"How not equal? Even I know that mending a plow blade is not detailed."

"He was doing repairs for a group of pilgrims who stopped in town. Heren told me Tonifee gave him a timeframe of a week to get the work finished, and he had to get his seeds in the ground before that. Coloy told him about me."

"I'll be sure to do something nice for Coloy as a way to thank her, then," Sara replied. "A nice wool scarf might be just the thing!"

"You? Knitting a scarf?"

"I'll mention it to Mum," Sara suggested. "She would want to find a way to thank Coloy for recommending you. She has always got random bits of yarn here and there, needing something to be done with them. It'd be a thrifty solution."

"That's a good thought, Sara," Pharis nodded her approval. "I don't know what the big secret is with the thread she has purchased."

"I have no idea, Pharis. She doesn't do much fine work that would require it, but there should not be any reason she is secretive about it."

"She is not going to tell us unless she decides to, or we stumble on whatever it is."

"That's not much of a surprise, really, sister mine."

"Doesn't make me stop being curious about it, though," Pharis replied, her voice soft. "I don't like secrets."

"I know you don't. I'm sure Mum has her reasons for keeping it quiet," Sara said. "Anyhow, I'm tired to my bones, and we have to get that axle mended for Rupert. Goodnight, Pharis."

"Goodnight, Sara. You did excellent work today, and I really do appreciate all your help in the smithy."

After having bid one another goodnight, the two young women lay in bed, thinking their own thoughts, until each fell asleep after their exhausting day. Isleni paused at their door, watching as her daughters slept, a fond smile blossoming on her tired face.

"Goddess keep you, my dears. Sleep well," she murmured to her slumbering daughters, then closed the door behind her and went to the soft warmth of her own bed.

5

Sara woke early before the sun had even begun its climb over the horizon and into the sky for the day. There was something wrong, but she could not quite put a finger on what that wrongness could be.

Pharis still slept, snoring softly in the pre-dawn darkness. She could hear one or two birds making tentative chirps outside, but nothing like the enthusiastic daytime discussions in which they engaged daily, once the waking sun began its inexorable rise into the sky.

Pulling on the clean but singed homespun tunic, leather trousers, and close-toed shoes that were her daily uniform in the smithy, Sara left the bedroom on tiptoe.

Islena lay in her glider dead asleep, her scrap-wool afghan sagging off her chest and pooling into her lap. Sara deftly rearranged the blanket, pulling it up under her mother's slight double chin. A soft smile blossomed on Isleni's pale face, one that Sara unconsciously echoed as she looked down at her sole remaining parent.

She took the remains of Isleni's final skein of yarn and placed it inside the basket that held scraps to be used another day.

Manu lay on his pallet near the woodstove, hand outstretched atop a piece of wood that waited to be added to the smoldering embers therein. He had nominated himself as the keeper of the nighttime fire upon his arrival, insisting that as he already slept in the front room, he was best able to keep an eye on things.

Sara gently moved the boy's fingers from the piece of wood and slid his slightly chilled hand beneath the lightweight-but-warm purple-and-green woolen afghan Isleni had crocheted for him upon his arrival. Manu had been overjoyed at Isleni's simple gesture, which had both warmed and embarrassed the kindhearted woman.

Sara placed the piece of firewood atop of the glowing embers, watching for a moment as wispy tendrils of smoke began to creep and rise from its now scorched exterior, before bursting into flame with a soft *whumph*! She closed the woodstove's door firmly, sealing it shut and keeping the hungry flames safe inside.

Sara grabbed a piece of soft fruit from the bowl on the kitchen table before going outside to see if whatever it was that had awakened her was still there. Were the birds so quiet because of whatever it was that was wrong or was it because it was still so dark outside?

Taking a bite of the slightly overripe fruit, Sara savored the sweet, thick juices that erupted from the orangey-yellow flesh within. The stone came free on its own, and she threw it into the lush grass at the side of the path she walked. Perhaps it would grow into a tree of its own. Maybe not, but it did not hurt to give it that opportunity instead of throwing it into the midden behind the house.

The recently shorn flock of sheep stared at her from their pen, with not even a blat, their strange, staring eyes giving no clue as to what was wrong. Knowing the beasts' natural avarice when it came to food, this only made Sara feel more concern.

Walking down to the forge, she checked and saw that the doors were still chained shut, and there was no sign of their having been disturbed. She heard something moving around behind the building, and it was all she could do to keep from screaming in shock and not a little fear.

A dragon stood behind the building, somehow managing to look lost, but when it laid eyes on her, it made an odd sound and came right up to Sara.

Its attitude was not threatening at all, and that was what kept Sara from running back to the house and locking herself in again. The dragon made a move as though to push its head against her chest, but after she experienced the slightest resistance, the solid-appearing head passed right through her, and it kept going.

Fighting the wave of dizziness that threatened to overcome her, Sara turned around and stumbled after the dragon. The human followed as the dragon led them down the hillside and toward the shoreline, where she was just able to make out a figure slumped on the ground near the water's edge.

Breaking into a run, Sara closed the distance in next to no time. Looking at the dragon who had guided her to this spot, she saw that it was becoming translucent, appearing ghostlier which each passing moment. A moan from the figure on the ground got her attention.

A dark oiled-leather helmet covered the Dragonguard's entire head, obscuring their eyes and most facial features, revealing only a well-shaped mouth and a slender, whiskerless chin.

Kneeling, Sara unbelted the snug chin strap and removed the helmet to reveal a young, blonde-haired woman, already-fair skin made paler by whatever it was that had laid her low now. The Dragonguard's eyelids fluttered open to reveal luminous golden-brown eyes. Sara noted in passing that what appeared to be a large quantity of hair was braided close to the young woman's scalp, kept under the concealing neutrality of the leather flying cap.

"Are you all right," Sara asked the woman, who stared up at her owlishly. "What can I do to help?"

"I need something to eat," she replied. "I was foolish and didn't bring enough with me."

"Food? You need food?" What did food have to do with whatever it was that was going on with her now? The young woman did not appear to be starving at the moment.

"Yes – please," the young woman whispered. "Whatever food you can find. I'm not picky."

Sara was running before she had even stood back up all the way, yelling for Manu as she returned to the house. The front door opened and he poked his head out when she was a dozen feet away.

"There's a Dragonguard down by the shoreline, Manu! Grab the loaf of bread and anything else you can find from the kitchen counter and take it down to her, along with something to drink. Do it now!" She grabbed the stout doorframe as she was almost brought to her knees by sudden, unexplained dizziness. "I'll be right behind you!"

Focusing hard on regaining her balance and then putting one foot in front of the other, she was just inside the house as Manu ran past her and outside, the half-eaten loaf of dark bread and what remained of a jug of sweet cider clutched in his hands. Sara saw that the dragon had followed her back to the house, and the beast was now leading the boy back to its stricken mistress.

A glance in the pantry showed her that it was time to visit the market in the village unless she wanted to dine on porridge for the day. A hard smoked sausage hung from a hook along the pantry wall, and she grabbed that to take down to the water's edge. A quick visual sweep of the kitchen area showed that there was little else available on short notice, and with a soft oath, she started toward the front door.

Another wave of vertigo overtook Sara, and she staggered, putting a hand on the kitchen table to steady herself. The table rocked a bit on its three-legged pedestal. The dizziness she felt frightened her. What was going on?

Sara felt as though her head was spinning, and she felt a bit sick to her stomach. Trying to call out, all that emerged from her mouth was an unintelligible mumble. Unaccountably weak, she collapsed to the floor, the world blurred, and then everything went black.

6

When Sara awoke, it was to find Manu kneeling next to her, trying to pour cooling water between her lips.

"Oh, Miss Sara! You're awake! Are you all right?" The relief on Manu's face was almost tangible. "Your Mum and sister have set off for the healer and left me here with you till they return. They couldn't get you to wake up. You scared all of us."

Sara tried to speak, but could not seem to get the breath to form words. It was as though she was exhausted to her very bones, but could think of no reason why that would be. Instead, she shook her head. For now, it was the only thing she could find the strength to do, and that weakness frightened her.

"Dragon."

"S'all right, Miss. The dragon showed me to its mistress, and I got her took care of. She is down by the creek now with a bit of the stew and pie from last night. S'cold, but I thought it would be okay for her. She gobbled that bread right fast and looked around for more."

"Good," she thought she had managed to say the word aloud, but could not be sure she had. It was becoming difficult to think. The world seemed to dissolve into patches of whiteness, and Sara wondered if she was dying. For some reason, the thought of that happening did not bother her.

Giving in to the returning wave of dizziness, Sara relaxed into whatever was overtaking her and allowed the blackness of deep sleep to overwhelm her once again. As long as the Dragonguard and her beautiful dragon were safe, Sara felt that that was enough.

Sara's Dreaming

It was as though her entire body was on fire, and she could do nothing to pull herself from the intense heat of flames that felt as though they charred her down to her nerve endings. A remote part of her mind, the part that was not screaming in agony, was reminded of the afternoon so long ago, when a drop of molten iron had burnt away the tip of the little finger on her left hand, the disfigured digit with its missing fingernail a constant reminder of the wages of inattention in dangerous circumstances.

Having done so in the past to escape bad dreams, Sara tried to wake herself, but this time, for what reason she could not guess, she remained trapped firmly in the consuming fires of her nightmare.

The ground beneath her feet cracked open to reveal molten rock flowing, and a scrap of unmelted land upon which she stood began to rock precariously.

She fell into the thick, boiling lava.

As Sara fought to escape her nightmare, the flames leaped higher and higher, and Sara felt her flesh curling off her limbs, leaving behind only blackened bone, but still, the agony continued.

Worry.

Anger.

Fear.

Hatred.

Loneliness.

All negative emotions were burned away from her as a feeling of belonging encompassed Sara's soul. The heat became something negligible, something meaningless, and so she embraced the fire and lava, stepping into the heart of the white-hot furnace at the center of her soul, welcoming it and then dismissing it with the barest flicker of thought.

Rest, said a rich voice that was neither male nor female, as actual sleep finally arrived. *I will watch over you.*

7

"**M**iss Sara, you must wake up! The dragon will not let us anywhere near you, and you must eat!" Manu's voice woke her. She had the feeling he had been yelling at her for some time now. How could a dragon that could not even touch you keep you away? "Miss Aya says you must wake up now!"

Miss Aya? Who was "Miss Aya"?

Sara opened her eyes.

There was not one dragon, but two, staring down at her. The second dragon was the color of fire, its scales colored red, orange, yellow, and blue, like the flames of the forge. Its long red tongue flicked out of its mouth, licking at Sara's cheek. This was something she was able to feel and in a way she did not at all expect.

She not only felt the dragon's tongue on her cheek but also had a sensation of touching scales on the end of her tongue.

"Odd feeling, isn't it?" said an unfamiliar voice from somewhere above the top of her head. "It took me awhile to get used to it and learn to tune it out."

Sara turned her head enough to see a young woman wearing what appeared to be soft leather riding clothes. Her platinum-blonde hair was plaited into a thick braid, the end of which was curled artfully out of the way at the nape of her neck.

The young woman wore what looked like a slender black suede scabbard strapped to her back, and Sara saw an odd-looking hilt of some delicate translucent object that was clearly not a sword sticking out of the thing. Whatever it was, it had not been the product of a forge and hammer.

"You're Aya?" she managed. Exhaustion she could not explain enveloped her mind and body. "I don't think I've ever seen you before."

"Yes, I am. Manu here tells me that your name is Sara. I tried talking to your mother about what was going on, but she was frightened and ran off with your sister. People tend to be frightened by the dragons, even though they should not be," the blonde girl explained kindly. "I'm not sure why young Manu did not follow them in their flight."

"Manu said they had gone off to find the healer. Did they?"

"Yes. I explained to her that you were fine and I would take care of you. That made her happy, and she went on her way. Your mother wasn't happy at all when I told her she should leave and take your sister with her. Sentinel had to encourage them to leave," Aya said. "I don't think your mother likes dragons very much."

"She doesn't. They scare her."

"Why do they scare her?"

"I have no idea," Sara replied. She looked at the flame-colored dragon again. "Where did the second dragon come from?"

"She is your dragon, Sara," Aya explained carefully. "You Dreamed her into existence, although from what I could see, it was more nightmare than a dream. That must have been very frightening. At least it seemed so by how much you writhed around while it happened."

The dragon in question came forward cautiously and then abruptly lay down, placing its head on Sara's chest. The creature's touch was somehow soothing, and Sara immediately relaxed.

"Eat this, Sara," Aya told her, pushing what appeared to be a bag of dried meat into her hand. "It will help you to recover. It will also keep your dragon in the physical realm."

Sara obediently put the first strip of pale yellow meat into her mouth and began to chew on it, finding that it tasted better than any meal she could ever remember having eaten. It was as though the sweet, dried squid was some sort of magical ambrosia, and she could not seem to get enough.

"I'm sorry it's not something better than dried squid, but it's all I was able to procure on short notice."

When the plain brown bread Manu handed her tasted just as enticing, she realized that something was very wrong. Her mother's bread, while quite good, was not something that was devoured.

"What's going on? I don't understand any of this!"

"I'm sorry this happened to you, Sara, but when you touched Sentinel, it activated whatever it is that causes a dragon to be Dreamed. Usually, it doesn't hit the new Dragonguard as quickly as it seemed to have hit you, so proper preparations can be made, and the arrival rendered as easy as it can be, under the circumstances."

"Sentinel? Is that your dragon's name?"

"Yes, that's her name," Aya replied with a smile, and the dragon under discussion flicked her tongue at Sara, her large, slit-pupiled eyes flashing copper and gold, which was odd, as they were not standing in sunlight. "It took me a long time to find out what it was, but it finally made itself known. We've been together now for a little over three years. It's been quite the adventure for us both, let me tell you, but the Dragonguard are like the family I never had, and I would not leave them for anything."

Sara had to chew up and swallow the big chunk of bread in her mouth, following it with a gulp of refreshing water before she could answer.

"I always thought dragons were larger than this. They certainly seem to be when I see the Dragonguard flying their patrols."

"Oh, they can be any size we want or need them to be, or even vanish, if necessary. For now, both dragons are smaller. This time, it was the only way to keep your family from being far more frightened than they already were. Frankly, I'm surprised Manu here did not follow them down the road."

As though responding to Aya's words, Sara's dragon shrank down to the size of a cat and climbed onto Sara's chest, pointed nose resting just below her chin. Reaching out a careful hand, she began to stroke the creature's scaled back, working to ignore the echo of her touch as she did so.

"Manu's not been right in the head since he survived a bout of the plague that took both his parents. He probably did not know he should be frightened." The subject of conversation did not even glance in their direction as he stroked the nose of Aya's Sentinel. Sara wondered how the interaction felt to Aya, as it was clear that Dragonguard and dragon were one and the same.

The dragon that was Sara's flicked out her tongue, the very tip of which connected with Sara's chin, making her flinch. A warm feeling that felt like a smile filled Sara's mind. The new dragon was pleased with itself.

"Do you know if there are Dragonguard in the boy's family?"

"No. I don't think so, anyway. Manu's parents were itinerant workers, going from farm to farm for work. I doubt that would be the case if there were Dragonguard in their lines." She took another sizeable strip of dried squid from the bag without comment, shoving it into her mouth and chewing for all she was worth.

"You'd be surprised," Aya replied dryly. "Anyway, Sentinel seems to think that there is every chance he may end up having a Dreaming. I'm concerned, as he may not have the mental capacity to endure something like that."

Sara gasped at the thought of that sweet-hearted child having to go through something like what she had just endured. Would he be able to survive something like that? But then, he had survived the plague, while his parents did not. Perhaps he was stronger than anyone realized, but at what price did that inner strength come?

"I suppose that if it happens, it happens," she finally said. "There would not be anything to stop it, would there?"

"No, there is not," Aya agreed. "We'll cross that bridge if we come to it, I suppose."

Sara looked at the boy who was quietly stroking Aya's dragon and sighed. Aya was right. There was nothing that could be done at this point. The child would survive, or he would not. There was nothing they could do to prevent it now.

"How long do you think he has before it happens?" Sara asked Aya.

"It's hard to tell. I lasted about half a day before it started for me, so I had time to eat and eat lots. Sentinel tells me that you passed out almost immediately after you touched one another. I'm assuming by how hard the Dreaming hit you that you had not eaten anything."

"I had a piece of fruit on my way out the door," Sara said, remembering the fruit that now seemed to have been part of a previous lifetime. "I've never been one to eat a big breakfast. My largest meal of the day is always dinner, and then a small supper after the day's work is done. I think I had finished the fruit before I saw your dragon."

"Well, now that you seem to be a bit more energetic, let's get you to your bed so you can get some rest. I would assume that your mother and sister will return shortly, with or without the authorities, although I don't know what they think the authorities could do with a Dragonguard and her dragon," Aya said, helping Sara to her feet. "Ready?"

Aya got Sara into her bed, with pillows stacked behind her so she could at least sit up comfortably. Sentinel and the new dragon shrank down to the size of large cats and joined Sara on top of the fluffy down comforter.

"The embroidery on this comforter is lovely," Aya exclaimed, bending over to peer at the splash of colors that decorated it. "Where did you get it?"

"My mother's mother made it for my sister and me when we were little. She collected the down from her own geese for three years until she had enough to make it," Sara explained. "She went through a lot of geese."

Both young women burst into laughter.

Anticipating what was to come, Aya dug out what food she could find in the pantry and fried up a stack of griddle cakes, sliced up some of the dense summer sausages Isleni always kept on hand and brewed up a pot of strong coffee to share. Once she had Manu situated at the table to devour what he had been given, she brought Sara's food to her where she lay in bed.

"Here you go, Sara," Aya said as she handed the wonderful-smelling breakfast over. "I can see by how he is eating that it probably will not be long until the boy starts his Dreaming. I'm thinking it would be better if that happened at the closest Dragonhold since they know how to handle it."

"Manu has always been a big eater so it may mean nothing at all," Sara suggested.

"That may well be, but nevertheless, it would be best if he was in Dragonhold hands if it is more than the hunger of a growing boy."

Sara took all this in as she stuffed her own mouth full of food. Who knew that producing something like a dragon could make one so voracious? Of course, who even knew how dragons came to be, other than those who possessed them?

Possessed.

No, that was a wrong word. It was clear now that there was no possession. No ownership. At its broadest, the unique split personality of it all should be called a partnership, as that appeared to be what it was; at its most unique, an additional limb. The now dog-sized dragon that lay at the foot of the bed raised her head and cocked it sideways.

"Someone's coming," Sara said to Aya, although she could see Aya already knew that. "My mother, maybe?"

The door burst open, and Isleni, Pharis, and Venton, the farmer from the next farm over, erupted into the front room, armed with crowbars and farm implements. What they saw brought them up short.

"What is going on here? Two dragons? Where did the second dragon come from?" Isleni demanded, rattled by what she was seeing.

"She is mine, Mum," Sara replied. "She is not going away."

Isleni gaped at her daughter, her mouth opening and closing like a landed fish, gasping for breath. Her gaze shot to the dragon that laid on her daughter's bed, and who was giving her full attention to the flustered woman.

"Don't let that thing near me," Isleni quavered, her tone of voice uncertain. "It's going to bite me, I know it!"

"It's not going to bite anyone here, Mum," Sara interjected with quiet certainty. She willed all the positive emotion she could into her thoughts and words, doing all she could to direct them into her mother's mind. "It's gentle, I promise."

Isleni's gaze went from her daughter and then back to the dragon, and her expression changed from fear to confusion.

"It has your eyes," Isleni said, almost too softly to hear. "How does it have your eyes? It's a giant lizard for the gods' sake! It's not possible."

Sara screwed up her courage. She knew her next words would not sit well with her mother. Not in the least.

"She is me, Mum."

Isleni's attention shot to her reclining daughter, and then back to the dragon. Confusion had now changed to anger.

"She is you? That doesn't make any sense, child, you must be delirious," she snapped. "It doesn't matter. You can't be a Dragonguard. This young woman can just take it back with her and find someone else to give the thing to! You need to stay here and help your sister."

Isleni gestured to Pharis as though inviting her to join the conversation, but Pharis did not say anything at all. Her expression showed that she did not necessarily agree with what her mother was saying. Did Pharis understand more than was apparent?

"I don't have any choice, Mum. She came from me and can't be taken back," Sara kept her voice quiet and calm, hoping that would calm her mother as well, but was promptly disappointed in that goal.

Isleni howled in anger, and Pharis put a restraining hand on her mother's shaking shoulder. While their mother was not at all a violent woman, who knew what might happen in this situation. She felt that one of her children was being threatened, and Isleni was not one to stand by while her child was in danger. She whirled to face the blonde young woman who stood watching the exchange between mother and daughter.

"You'll take this thing back with you now young lady!" she demanded of Aya, who until this time, had not spoken a word. Sara saw her sister squeeze her mother's shoulder. Knowing that her mother otherwise had nothing but reverence and praise for those who rode dragons, Sara was shocked by her mother's temerity when face to face with one of their number.

"She is telling you the truth, Mistress," Aya replied politely, showing no anger in her voice and facial expression. Sara imagined this might be a common occurrence with the Dragonguard when confronting families about the Dreaming of new dragons. "There is no going back where the dragon is concerned. The dragon was inside your Sara all along and has chosen to emerge into the outer world. Your daughter and her dragon-self are together forever, and there is nothing I could do to change that, even if I wanted to do so."

Flustered, Isleni wrenched herself free of Pharis' restraint and took a step forward, but Venton moved in front of her, blocking her way. He turned to face the angry woman.

"Mistress Isleni, my late wife's younger cousin Veronin is a Dragonguard. This young lady speaks the truth. There is nothing that will part them now. Accept this and move on with your life," the farmer told her firmly. "You have your daughter and the boy. They will have to sustain you."

Perhaps it was because someone who was not a Dragonguard had spoken, Isleni's fearsome expression shattered into one of grief.

She burst into tears and fell into Venton's arms. Although the normally taciturn man seemed embarrassed at Isleni's emotional breakdown, he kept the stricken woman from falling to the floor.

"There is more, Mistress, though I hate to add to your unhappiness," Aya continued. "The boy may shortly have the same thing happen to him, and it is in his best interest that I take him to the nearest Dragonhold before that happens. I promise that he will be well taken care of there. If he does not gain a dragon of his own, I will bring him back as soon as is possible."

"Don't let them benefit from him, Sara! You know how special he is!" Isleni cried out, glaring daggers at the platinum-haired Dragonguard.

"I am very well aware of that, Mum," Sara replied. "I promise that I will watch out for him."

Sara's dragon slid down from the bed and approached Isleni. The woman quailed at the creature's approach, then straightened, staring up at the dragon defiantly.

"What do you want? Why did you come here," she demanded hoarsely, as though expecting an answer from the creature. "Why didn't you choose another rider instead of my Sara? You've ruined my family!"

The dragon reached out a paw to touch Isleni, then seemed to think better of it and instead sat back on her haunches, content just to look at the small angry woman. The beast gave low musical chirp and turned her gaze to Pharis, whose expression held wonder, rather than anything resembling fear.

Sara, lowering her hand to her side, felt an odd juxtaposition in her mind, as the dragon's mind and her own mind went their own directions. From the corner of her eye, she saw Pharis looking from the dragon to her, but did not let on that she had noticed.

Watching the flame-colored beast, Sara could tell that the dragon refused to be intimidated by Isleni, and was happy the creature had not chosen to make herself even larger to prove some kind of a point. Isleni was angry, and when she was angry, she did not always respond as one might expect.

"Mistress, I would take the boy with me now, and leave your Sara here overnight to rest before I return to take her to the Aerie. Would that be acceptable to you?" Aya interceded, stepping between the livid woman and the dragon. "There is a chance that Manu here won't end up with a dragon of his own, but it's best to discover such a thing in the safety of the Dragonhold."

"I suppose I don't really have a choice, do I?" Isleni replied, her voice sullen as a spoiled child's. It did not suit her. "You'll have the dragon flame me if I try to stop you."

"The Dragonguard doesn't do any such thing, Mistress," Aya replied, shocked at Isleni's accusation. "Right now, the Aerie is the best and safest place for her to be until she and her dragon become better acquainted. I promise you, she will return to visit, in time."

"So what am I supposed to do until you return for my daughter," Isleni demanded.

"Don't touch the dragon," Aya advised and stared hard at Sara, as though trying to tell her something. What could be wrong with touching the dragon? It was not as though the creature was dangerous. "There might be odd side effects if you do."

"I certainly won't be touching it, young lady and Pharis will go nowhere near the thing!" Isleni snapped, her defiance returning. "Will I need to feed the beast before you return? I have no desire to be devoured."

"She will take care of herself, Mistress," she told Isleni. "You don't have to worry about feeding her at all. Just make sure that Sara has plenty to eat until I return."

"Sara can fend for herself. She is as old as I was when I married her father. Pharis and I will be leaving now, and I will not return until this beast is gone from my home."

Isleni turned away and then turned back again. The anger was gone from her face, replaced with curiosity.

"I recall that dragons are much larger. How long will it be until the beast gets its full growth?"

"She can be any size she wishes, Mistress," Aya said brightly. "For now, she chooses to be smaller, so she does not inconvenience you any more than is necessary."

"Interesting," was Isleni's flat reply as she turned away again and then swept out the door without another word, closing it behind her. Pharis, following her mother, put her fingertips on the doorknob, then dropped her hand. She turned to Sara with a broad smile.

"I guess you just might find the husband you wanted," she blurted. "Congratulations, sister, on your new friend. Never forget that I love you, Sara. Mum does, too. She is just in a twist for now. Try to forgive her."

And then Pharis left.

A moment later, the farmer popped his head in and gave a shy smile at both Sara and the dragon.

"Congratulations, Miss Sara, on your dragon. I'll keep the two of them at my place until you're able to go, ladies. I know my cousin told me more than he should have, but I'll keep them both as safe as I'm able," and he went away.

8

"But why must I go with her," Manu asked reasonably. "I should keep an eye on you until Mistress Isleni returns."

"Manu, things have changed, and it's important that you go with Aya. It's okay. She will keep you safe," Sara assured the troubled child. "Just go with her."

"The Mistress with be angry with me if I leave you alone," Manu wailed. His dark skin had an unusually pale cast to it, and Aya knew that he had to go and go now.

"No, Manu, she knows you'll be going with Aya and that I'll follow along soon. Please trust me on this," Sara begged him. "Everything will be all right."

The boy drew himself up in righteous indignation, and Sara knew from previous experience that there was nothing for it but to take direct action.

Looking at Aya, she said in a low but firm voice, "Please take him right now."

Nimble on her feet, the Dragonguard grabbed the boy and hauled him outside, her dragon following along behind her. Manu's startled protests changed to shrieks of anger, and then there was blessed silence. Sara hoped his silence had come from passing out from exhaustion but knew there was a chance he had been rendered senseless to make transporting the boy easier on Aya.

"Come here, dragon," Sara said, and the creature came back to her, growing in size a bit as she did so. By the time she reached the bed, she was the size of a small draft horse and had to keep her head down to avoid hitting it on the beams that supported the ceiling. "Let's cuddle up."

Once at Sara's bedside, the dragon lay down once more, resting her head on Sara's chest. If someone had asked her to describe the sensation, she would have told them that it felt *right* but would not have been able to tell them why.

The contact also made Sara realize how tired she really was. Her eyes slowly shut, and she fell back to sleep, knowing she was safe with the flame-colored dragon watching over her as she slept.

Sara's dreams were of flying, although she could not tell if she was herself or the dragon, as she soared through the purple and blue night sky, looking down at the land and its inhabitants' dwellings below, their tiny flickering windows lit by the fires and candles within. Sometimes she would race up high into the air, while at others, she would very nearly kiss the ground, zooming along as the drying tops of the nearly-ripe grain tickled her belly scales. It was a feeling she had never before known existed and reveled in the experience.

For a little while, sized down to match, she and a hunting owl engaged in a race through the trees, a contest which only came to an end when a fat, dozing squirrel was knocked into their path, and the owl used that opportunity to capture a satisfactory meal. Disinterested in food as she had no need or desire to eat, Sara tipped her snout to the feathered predator and left him to his feast.

While Sara was aware the air was cooling the higher she rose, it did not make her at all uncomfortable. At some point, she realized that she could no longer hear the sounds of earth or sky or even noise of flapping dragon wings. There was only the sound of the wind's companionable presence as she swept up and through the moisture-soaked clouds, to see only a crisp black sky full of planets and stars overhead.

Sara continued her aerial ballet for quite some time, diving into and out of the dense, rain-bloated clouds until she became aware of herself rousing from sleep, and she rushed back to her rousing self, still wrapped in her down comforter. Once again inside her house, she shrank down to the size of a large housecat and jumped onto the bed to stare down at herself as she opened her eyes to see herself looking down at her.

"Oh, hello there," Sara said to the dragon who gave her a toothy yawn in reply. "Did we really do that?"

The dragon, of course, said nothing but curled up under her chin, her tiny, jewel-like scales coldish and soothing against Sara's slumber-warmed flesh. Reaching up with tentative fingers, she gently stroked the beast who was also, somehow, herself and once again marveled at feeling both slick scales and soft flesh at the same time.

Scratching gently at the base of one of the dragon's wings, Sara became aware of the fact that she itched in precisely that location on her own body, although having no wings herself, it was her shoulder blades that required attention.

A little further experimentation with strategic scratching resulted in success at ridding herself of that discomfort. What an odd but beautiful side effect of Dreaming one's own dragon!

After lying in bed for a while longer, Sara got up, made a rude breakfast from a piece of the ever-present hard cheese in the cupboard and a thick slice of yesterday's loaf of dark bread. As she munched, Sara grabbed a rucksack and began to pack those things she thought she might need in her new home. If she missed anything, it would be fast and easy to retrieve.

Her best brush was packed away once she had tidied her hair and bound it into a neat bun at the crown of her scalp. She then added a pair of tunics, some trousers, her only decent skirt, and a frilly whatnot of a blouse that had rarely seen wear, but why take the chance of not having something beautiful in the event it was necessary.

Sara was fussing over miscellaneous toiletries when Aya returned. The rucksack had been filled to the point of being overstuffed, and she had dug out an old, worn canvas bag for whatever else she wished to pack.

"Whatever you don't have with you can easily be gotten at the Aerie," Aya told Sara as she looked at the bulging bags. "There's no need to worry overmuch. What did you have for breakfast this morning?"

"Some cheese and bread," Sara answered, turning back to her packing. "I don't eat much in the morning."

"That's not enough, Sara," Aya chided her. "You need to be eating at least enough to make your belly feel a bit more than full."

"I can't eat that much! I'll blow up like a fish's swim bladder!"

"Trust me, Sara, you won't get fat. It requires a lot of food to keep your dragon solid enough to ride," Aya laughed. "You keep packing your things, and I'll cook up something for you."

A short time later, Sara sat down to a heaping plate of eggs, sausage, more of the hard cheese, now melted across the plate, and fried potatoes. It was, she knew, more than she could eat, but she dutifully applied herself to the meal.

"Wait a minute, I don't remember having sausages like this in the cupboard," Sara exclaimed through a mouthful of half-chewed sausage.

"I brought them from the Aerie," Aya told her with a smile. "Adalena insisted I bring some with me 'for the new Dragonguard.'"

"How is Manu? Was his Dreaming difficult on him?"

"It seems he is not due to join our numbers, so in a few days, after we feed him up a bit and our medics see to some issues they found, he will be returned here."

For some reason, this news pleased Sara, but she only smiled and finished off the last of the heavily seasoned but tasty sausages.

"That said, there is something special about him that caught Sentinel's attention, so we'll be keeping an eye on the boy," Aya continued. "We don't want to lose track of him."

"Special? Oh yes, he is special," Sara agreed. "The boy remembers anything he hears. The unfortunate part of that he is simple-minded. We're afraid if someone else discovers that, they'll take him away and do something terrible to him."

"Ah, well, then, he might be safer in the Aerie than here in the landbound world," Aya suggested, with a thoughtful expression. "All the dragons seem to like him, so he would not be out of place. I'll talk with Mikkel about what we can do."

"Mikkel?"

"He is sort of a father figure for the youngsters in the Aerie. I think you'd like him," Aya suggested.

"I'm not looking for a father," Sara blurted, angry. "I had a father!"

"No, not as a father, and before you say anything else a lover, either. He is just a very good man. His dragon is called Sky."

"Sky? How do you know a dragon's name?"

"You come up with it on your own. At some point, the appropriate name will come to you, and then that will be her name forever. Take your time. There are not any rules about when that has to happen. Anyhow, he will help you learn how to be a Dragonguard, and what you need to know to keep the both of you safe when you're flying."

"Speaking of flying, my dragon went out last night and flew around, and I saw it all happening while I slept!"

"That's normal, especially when you're first becoming accustomed to your dragon. You're the same person, really, but in some ways, your dragon also wants to be herself. Some like to explore more than most. Sentinel wasn't much."

The dragons in question were both curled up on Sara's bed, eyes closed. Sara knew hers was not actually sleeping but was merely biding her time until called upon to do something.

Sara's eyes fell on the scabbard on Aya's back, and her curiosity about it returned.

"What's that on your back, Aya? It doesn't look like a sword."

"It's not. It's a staff of sorts, I suppose. I found it a little while before I Dreamed Sentinel. All I know is that it is the horn of a *vaasa*."

"A *vaasa*? What's that?"

"I've never seen one, myself, but my father, Drannar told me that they are very rare one-horned beasts that live in the otherwise uninhabited parts of the world that possess much magic in the land, plants, and trees. Hornsmiths work them into staves like mine."

"May I see it?"

Aya looked uncomfortable and made a face.

"I keep it with me as much to know where it is as to keep anyone from touching it accidentally. *Vaasahorn* has a bad habit of killing those who try to take it without asking," she explained. "I simply decided to not let anyone touch it at all, and then I don't have to worry about it."

"How can a piece of horn kill with a mere touch?"

"I don't know the magic behind it, but that's what happens," Aya replied her voice firm. "You can imagine that I have no desire to test it myself."

"I can't imagine that you would," Sara agreed. "I don't understand it, though."

"I don't either, Sara," Aya told her. "I simply accept what I have been told, in addition to seeing the reaction of those who see it and who knows what it is."

Sara nodded.

"Anyhow, write a note to your mother and sister, telling them that you've gone and that you'll be back when you can. I don't want either of them thinking you've been kidnapped and will never see either of them again," Aya suggested with a soft chuckle. "I've seen a 'rescue party' try to attack an Aerie in the past when they did not believe what they were told."

"Do you see your family?"

"My mother is dead, and my brother ran off," Aya said, her expression abruptly going blank. "My only family is in the Aerie now."

"What about your father? You said something about your father before."

"I killed the man who sired me," Aya responded. "I was adopted by one of the Dragonguard, not too long after my arrival there. Drannar is far more deserving of my loyalty and love than Andagebi ever was."

The level of hate Sara saw on Aya's face was beyond anything she had ever before seen in her life, almost tangible in its power. She hoped never to see hatred like that aimed at her.

"Why did you kill him?" There was no accusation or judgment in Sara's question. Whatever had happened, there was something that made her certain that Aya's actions were justified.

"He murdered my mother and newborn baby sisters and would have murdered me if he had had the chance, I think."

"Why didn't the local Justice do something about that," Sara demanded, shocked at what she had been told. "You can't just murder people! There are laws against that sort of thing!"

"I come from a country far from yours, where my father had every right to do what he did. The male head of the household can do what he wishes where his family is concerned, especially with the women, who have no say in their lives."

Sara recalled stories about such things but had discounted them as fairy stories used to make children behave. To discover there was truth in those stories was something that brought her grief for those girls and women who suffered that existence.

Sara hoped she would never find a reason to visit the blonde girl's childhood country. While she knew that having a dragon would keep anyone there from doing her harm, she did not trust herself not to do harm to those who lived there.

"You say you have a brother. Does he know what you did," Sara asked, grateful for the distraction from her dark thoughts. "How could anyone accept their mother's murder at the hands of their own father?"

"I have no idea, and I really don't care. My brother watched while my father beat my mother bloody and at some point, left," Aya said, her voice thickening with the power of her emotion, Sentinel's eyes opened from where she lay on the bed, staring at her human half. "He did not do anything to stop what my father did. When my mother Zoraya refused to consider the marriage he had arranged for me, he beat her to death. Instead of stepping in to stop Andagebi from killing her, my brother Gebi turned coward and ran away."

Sara saw tears welling up in Aya's eyes and passed her a clean handkerchief from her pocket. To give the Dragonguard a chance to regain her composure, Sara rose and began to clean up. In the length of time it took her to get the kitchen tidy and compose the requested letter of farewell, the blonde young woman had dried her eyes and appeared ready to leave.

"Let's get your things together and leave, Sara. As I said earlier, you can easily retrieve anything you might have forgotten, if not replace it entirely at the Aerie. We are a somewhat self-sufficient people."

"I wanted to ask you about that, Aya," Sara said. "I've always heard the place where the Dragonguard reside called the Dragonhold. Why do you call it the Aerie?"

"The Dragonhold is the term that most land-bound folks are accustomed to for those places. Some of us call them that, while others, including myself, call them Aeries. It's up to you what you call it. Neither is incorrect. For me, I just like the word "Aerie" better, I suppose."

"How many Dragon...uh...Aeries are there?"

"Twenty-three, at last count," Aya told her, picking up one of the two well-stuffed bags and slinging it over one shoulder. Sara grabbed the other, leading the way toward the front door. "There are at least two per country, if not more. It depends on that country's needs. Yours has two at the moment."

Sara stopped and turned to look at what had been her home, heaving a great sigh. She could describe every room and item in it from her lifetime of memories, walk through it all, eyes closed, and never bump into anything along the way.

The compact kitchen was immaculate, every bed made, and a pile of cut and split firewood filled the shallow wicker basket near the wood stove almost to overflowing. Sara's note was on the kitchen table, propped up against a medium-sized bowl full of the tasty hard-smoked sausages Aya had brought with her from the Dragonhold.

Her dragon nudging her from behind, Sara turned to face the world ahead of her, the sun's position in the sky showing that it was nearly noon on the first day of the rest of her life. What new surprises awaited her today?

9

"Just climb onto her back and hold on," Aya advised Sara after several minutes of false starts from the nervous young woman. "She is not going to let you fall off."

"That's easy for you to say," Sara protested. "You've got how many years of experience now, flying a dragon?"

"Three, but that's not my point," Aya retorted.

"I'm new to this. I have a difficult enough time riding our lazy old plowhorse!"

"You're being silly, Sara," Aya chided the younger girl. "We have to go, and that's not going to happen unless you get on her back and we leave. Believe me, it's better for everyone if you go. Even though dragons keep the world a safer place, most folks are frightened of them. Sometimes, that fright can lead to bad things."

"I'm going to miss my family!" she protested. "I don't want to go in the first place! It's crushing my heart even to think of leaving them. Why do you want that?"

"I know you'll miss them, Sara, but it's better for them, *for now*, for us to be on our way. You can come visit them later. You're not a prisoner, after all."

Taking a sobbing breath and standing up straighter, Sara put a hand on her dragon, the skin to scale contact helping to steady her emotions.

The flame-colored beast waited while Sara got on and settled herself behind the dragon's wide shoulders. She had one bag strapped to her back, and Aya had fastened the other to what had been an unoccupied metal ring on the leather harness strapped around her own dragon.

"Now, take a deep breath, and think *up*," the blonde woman told Sara. "Remember to brea—"

And then they were airborne, and Sara gasped, looking down at the world as details dwindled in size, the dragon's great wings cupping the air as she moved upward and away from the hard ground.

"Different, isn't it," Aya asked her once they'd reached a certain point of height. "It still seems like magic to me."

"I never imagined things looked like this from up in the sky," Sara replied. "Things look so small down there."

"When regular people run out and stare up at us, they look like dolls or ants, depending on how high you've flown," Aya observed, and then pointed to the east. "See the trading caravan heading up into the mountains?"

"Yes."

"They're not what they seem," Aya told her. "I've got it on good authority that they're smuggling goods into other countries."

"They've got illegal things in their wagons? Shouldn't we do something about that," Sara demanded.

"I should clarify that they're illegal in countries they plan to visit," Aya said. "They're perfectly legal here in this country."

Sara was confused and said as much.

"They're bringing goods in that for one reason or another are not legal in those other countries," Aya told her. "There may or may not be a good reason for that, but I believe that the intent of the caravanners is not ill. As it is, we Dragonguard turn a blind eye to their activities, unless they begin to trade in legitimately illegal items."

They flew for a long time in silence before Sara asked the question that had been foremost in her thoughts almost since her Dreaming.

"Why does the Dreaming have to be so awful? I thought I was dying!"

"Everyone's Dreaming is different. Some are peaceful and calm, while others are more painful and violent," Aya said, raising her voice a bit to be heard over the sound of the wind. "I'm assuming yours was painful."

"Yes. Wasn't yours?"

"No, mine wasn't. I'm sorry that yours wasn't that way. What happened in yours?"

"I burned. Every last bit of me was on fire. A fire that could not be quenched."

Aya was quiet for a time, as though digesting that single word. Sara wondered what the blonde woman's Dreaming had entailed.

"That must have been terrible, Sara," Aya finally said. "I wish I could have made it easier for you, but that's not possible. Everyone's Dreaming is what it is."

Sara thought about what Aya told her and felt grief and sadness she could not explain. The agony she had felt was something that seemed extreme and terrible, but she realized something else.

"I guess that as bad as it was, I would experience the same thing if it still led to my Dreaming of something...someone...as as wonderful as my dragon."

"That's exactly it, Sara," Aya replied. "Others with whom I have spoken about their own Dreaming have said almost exactly the same thing you have."

The rest of their flight continued in silence, as each replayed their own Dreamings in their heads.

Taking the letter from her weeping Mother's shaking hand, Pharis read the note Sara had left, her sister's otherwise neat handwriting in the rich brown ink smeared with what must have been the tears she had shed while composing it.

Dearest Mum and Sister:

I'm sorry to have to leave now, but I have been convinced that it is for the best. I won't be completely gone from your lives, as I will visit as much as I am able.

I believe I have packed all I will need to have with me as I join the Dragonguard, but if I discover a need for something I left behind, I have been assured that that item will be made available to me at the Aerie. That said, I have left some things for you both as mementos of me on the bed. There is a note with each pile that explains to whom each belongs.

I ask that you honor this.

I will miss you both so very much. I hope that you can eventually understand and support what I have done today. Be assured that this is not a funeral, but a new beginning for me.

The Dragonguard Aya, rider of Sentinel, both of whom you met today, tells me that if you were to post a letter to me, it would be delivered shortly to me, at whatever Aerie I might be in at that time.

All my love, your daughter, and sister,

Sara

PS: Telling Garland that you have a Dragonguard in the family might make him more predisposed to prompt and polite payment. Take advantage of it!

10

The Aerie

"**D**iscovered her name yet?" Mikkel asked Sara over breakfast, three days after her arrival at Golden Aerie, which was about a score of leagues from her family home, covered in a few hours of lazy dragon flight. The girl shook her head, mouth full of scrambled eggs and sausage, too polite to speak while chewing on a mouthful of food. "No hurry, I was just curious."

Sara swallowed and took a sip of her strong black tea before she answered. She preferred the leafy brew, sweetened with a dollop of honey to the coffee that was also available.

"I don't want to just come up with a name off the top of my head. This is something serious to me," she protested. "I mean, it is not as though she is a puppy or a kitten, after all!"

"Of course it's serious, I just meant..."

"Can you imagine someone calling their dragon something like Spot or Fang?"

"Kendall's dragon is called Spot," Mikkel told her dryly. "They're at Brydon Aerie. You'd understand why he is called that if you saw him."

"Really? Spot? Why?"

"Kendall survived a terrible bout of smallpox as a child, but not without lifelong evidence of that fact. His Dreaming had a sense of humor."

"What does one have to do with the other?"

"Haven't you wondered why others' dragons are the colors and patterns they are? It has to do with their human selves. My Sky is colored the way he is because of the things I liked to do even before I touched Darkness and had my Dreaming. No two dragons are colored precisely alike, just as no two humans are exactly alike."

"Darkness? I haven't met that dragon yet."

"You'll not meet Darkness or her rider, Evani until you pass into the next life. We lost them both a dozen years ago," Mikkel told her, voice tight with remembered pain. "It was a terrible thing."

"I'm sorry for your loss," Sara said automatically. Mikkel stared at her, startled out of his memories. Sara could see the tears brimming in his eyes.

"You have no idea. Evani was more than the dragon that brought me Sky, she was my best friend," he murmured, then took a loud, deep breath. "Please excuse me, I've some things that need tending to this morning."

He stood, his breakfast platter dressed in no more than the barest fragments of the extensive breakfast he had devoured. Sara had long ago noticed that the Dragonguard were not ones to leave food behind when they left the table.

"Finish your meal and then go meet with Barlay," he told Sara gruffly, dashing the tears from his eyes with a forefinger. "He wants to discuss something with you but wants you to eat your fill, first. I've noticed you still eat as though you're not yet a Dragonguard. It's not as though you're going to get plump, you know. Have you ever seen a fat Dragonguard in your life?"

Sara choked on the sip of tea she had been drinking, and Mikkel pounded on her back to help, offering apologies as he did so.

"N-no," she allowed once she got her breath back. "I guess I'm just too used to eating like a regular person."

"Can't do that, lass," he reminded her, patting her shoulder. "Don't you ever forget that. Remember that Aya ended up on your doorstep as it were because she did not eat enough that day."

"Well, that wasn't a bad thing, really," Sara replied. "If she had eaten enough, I'd never have Dreamt my beautiful girl!"

"There is that, of course, but we're not out there trying to increase our numbers. We've got more than enough Dragonguard in the Aeries for now."

"How many Aeries are there?"

"Twenty-seven at last count, with two in the making. Two hundred souls average, per Aerie, so roughly five thousand Dragonguard having to support ourselves across the world. There is only so much arable land out there that's available to us, and we can only produce so much a year."

"Don't the Aeries ask for tithes? Some of the folk I know have told me that soldiers will come to their homes and farms demanding tithes in the name of the Dragonguard."

"Wait a minute. Landsmen have been demanding goods and services from people in our name?" Mikkel's expression was a mix of consternation and fury. Whatever his earlier claimed errand bad been now forgotten. "When did this happen last?"

"A pair of men went to Orton's farm just after the Fall harvest, demanding a wagonload of wheat and oats."

"Orton, you say," Mikkel said. "I must get this information to the Greater Council as soon as possible. If you would excuse me."

"Of course," she managed and watched as the man began to stride away. Then he stopped in his tracks, turning back to look at her.

"The Greater Council may wish to speak with you on this matter, Sara. If you can, please try to make a list of others you know have been affected by these robberies." Anger burned in the man's eyes. "I wish we had learned about this earlier. I suppose that is what happens when we tend to fill our numbers primarily from among our existing community. We need to become less aloof."

"Yes, I will," Sara assured him, nodding her head. With that, Mikkel continued on his way.

"Can you imagine the reaction if we tried doing something like that? People have a difficult enough time making ends meet without having to fill *our* empty stomachs. We feed ourselves at our own expense," Aya, who had walked up near the end of Sara and Mikkel's conversation, suggested. "From what I heard you say, this is going to get ugly. Whoever these so-called soldiers are, they have nothing to do with the Dragonguard. We barter for and purchase our own food."

"So the Dragonguard farm?"

"Yes, some do, if they've the green thumb to do so. I've given the Dragonguard what land my family had, once I joined them. It's not much, but it's good for raising grains, melons, and hogs. That's what my family grew before I dreamed Sentinel. The family that works it now are the son and daughter of Dragonguards. Neither had the whatever it is someone needs to Dream a dragon, so they do what they can to help support our communities."

"That must have been a welcome addition for getting food, then," Sara said. "It's sort of funny how much I think about it now."

"That's not a bad thing, Sara. In fact, I'm sure you've discovered that food tastes even better now than it did before."

"I hadn't thought of that, but yes, you're right," Sara replied. "Is it because of the Dreaming?"

"I think it's your body and mind trying to get you to eat as much as possible to keep your connection with your dragon-self strong. People tend to have more of an appetite when the food tastes good," Aya suggested. "Of course, things that already taste good now taste wonderful!"

"I need to get you to Barlay, Sara. Are you done eating now?"

Sara looked at her empty plate, amazed at the sheer amount of what she had consumed. She looked back at Aya.

"I suppose I am."

"Where is Manu?" Sara asked, realizing she had not laid eyes on her foster brother since he left her old home.

"Your Manu is an enigma, Sara. While he did not Dream, he seems to have some sort of a connection to dragons.

"It was decided that he be moved to an Aerie several hundred score leagues from here. It was best, Barlay and the rest of the Council decided, to take him somewhere he was not known by others. He is fine where he is, for now at least."

Sara felt sad, which was unexpected for her.

"I'd hoped to see him," she admitted. "He is a reminder of home."

"It's best if he gets used to being part of an Aerie as soon as possible. He will be fine. Stardust Aerie has excellent facilities for those who are like Manu."

"When would I be able to see him, then?"

"I'd give him a few months to get settled, he can be assessed and put in the best situation for his needs. I assure you, as I did with your mother, that we will protect him from those who would exploit his unique talent."

"If you think that's best, I'll stay away for now," Sara replied, "but I won't stay away forever."

"I'd think less of you if you did," Aya said with a smile. "I know you only want what's best for him."

"I did not think I could become attached to him, and I'm sort of surprised that I have. We took him in because he needed help and we needed the help and could afford to support him, so we volunteered to do just that."

"I wish I could have had a relationship like that with my brother, but I did not. The country I come from discourages closeness between the sexes, even between family members. As it is, because of how my mother died, I don't really want to ever see him again."

"What you've told me about your relationship with your brother and your father is entirely the opposite of my relationship with my family. Yes, my father would have loved to have had a son, but I think he was thrilled when my sister not only showed an aptitude for smithing but actually wanted to follow in his footsteps. He never so much as suggested she was making a wrong choice. No, he encouraged her to do whatever it was she wanted to do with her life that would make her happy. The idea of roles based strictly on gender is not right, to my way of thinking."

"I have wondered where I would be now if I had been raised in a more open and welcoming environment than I was," Aya said. "Would I have even had the opportunity to become one of the Dragonguard? That's a question that can never be answered, but it's also one that doesn't go away."

"Well, unless someone discovers that dragons have hidden talents as yet undiscovered, that is the case."

"So, are you done stuffing your face?" Aya asked her friend, eyeing the bare dusting of food crumbs scattered across Sara's platter.

"I couldn't eat another bite," Sara replied, wiping her mouth. "Let's go see Barlay!"

11

"Mikkel and Aya have told me that you appear to be settling in nicely here in the Aerie, Sara," the old Dragonguard said with a warm smile. "Is there anything you think I should know about? We want you to be comfortable in your new life with us."

"So far, everything is fine, my lord," Sara replied. "Once I made my preferences known to the quartermaster, I was given quarters with plenty of bright areas and a study where I can work on other things when I'm not on Dragonguard duty."

"Good, good," Barlay replied, still smiling. "I'm very pleased to hear that! Have you had much opportunity to fly your dragon since you arrived?"

"Goodness, no," Sara said. "I've been kept fairly busy with outfitting, moving into my quarters, and poring through the regulations I must follow in my new vocation."

"Vocation, eh? I like the sound of that," the old man laughed, his dark eyes twinkling. The ghostly white dragon on his shoulder rearing to his hind legs and making a tinny bugle. "Makes us sound like a bunch of fussy old monks and nuns!"

"Fussy, my lord?" Aya chuckled. "I prefer the word *dedicated* if you please."

"Fine, *dedicated*, then, child," Barlay grinned at the two young women. "Wouldn't want to disappoint you, would I?"

"Was there anything else, then, my lord," Sara asked. "I know you are busy today with more important things than seeing that I'm comfortable. I don't want to delay your day any longer."

"Oh, bother that, child," was his reply. "I also wanted to ask you to come along with me today. Good practice for riding your dragon, and we can get to know one another better!"

Sara's heart raced a bit at his request but was wise enough not to demur.

"Of course, my lord!" She responded. "May I go to the kitchens to get some food for the both of us to eat during our flight?"

"Ah, capital! You've been paying attention to your lessons! Yes, please go to Mireya and ask her to provide you with two packages of travel food and be sure to mention my name when you do. I have some food sensitivities, so she has to make sure I only get things I can eat," Barlay told her. "Be off with you now! I'll be ready to leave on the half hour. Meet me on the plateau just before then."

Bowing politely before leaving, the two young women made their way to Sara's quarters, where she began changing into her riding clothes. She reached for the warmer of her two riding jackets, but Aya stopped her.

"Take the lighter one, Sara. In fact, put a tunic on under your riding jerkin and tuck it into your trousers," she advised. "Better to layer your clothing that way. It's not quite cool enough out right now to worry about warmer clothing. It will be soon, but not yet. Enjoy that while you can."

Aya reached into the small closet that housed Sara's tunics and gowns and pulled out a vivid yellow cotton tunic that the tailor had insisted Sara use, once she saw the girl's dragon. The yellow reminded Sara of the color of a fresh egg from one of her family's fat brown hens.

"Here. This should look spectacular on you," the platinum-haired young woman told Sara. "Might as well show off a bit when meeting new people, right?"

Sara pulled off the off-white tunic she had been wearing and substituted the yellow one. Looking at herself in the mirror that hung on one wall, she was forced to agree that it was both attractive and striking.

"I'll go get the food packages for you and Barlay. Take the time to brush out your hair and braid it. Flying tends to encourage nasty tangles, especially with curly hair like yours, and unless you decide to cut your hair short, you're going to have to get used to doing that." Aya put a hand to her own thick braid and pulled it over her right shoulder. "It's a pain in the arse, but I like having long hair, so I live with the inconvenience of it all. Anyhow, I'm off. I'll meet you on the plateau in fifteen minutes."

Once Aya was gone, and the door closed tight, Sara braided her thick hair into a fuzzy braid, and then took a moment to look at herself once again in the mirror. She rarely took time to assess her personal appearance, but for now, it seemed to be appropriate.

The corset-like black riding jerkin, with its internal steel boning, was a stark contrast to the vivid egg-yolk yellow of the poufy-sleeved tunic that rested on the edges of her shoulders, revealing the delicate outline of her breastbone. The skin-tight riding trousers were comfortable against her skin, with the knee-high, brass-ringed riding boots laced snugly over them.

Snagging her riding helmet from its perch on the mirror's corner as she turned away from her reflection, Sara left the room, the dragon fluttering along behind her, obligingly cat-sized to prevent their quarters from being too cramped to move around in.

Sara walked for a few hundred feet before she realized she was stupid. Coming to an abrupt halt, she waited for her dragon to come alongside her and then climbed up onto the broad, smooth-scaled shoulders, and bracing herself for the dragon's leap into the air. Once airborne, it was less than a minute before she reached the plateau, Aya, and the broadly grinning Barlay already there, awaiting her arrival.

"Glad to see you realized you did not have to walk it," Barlay laughed when she landed. "I think I was halfway up the path before I realized I was doing things the hard way."

"So this was some sort of a test, was it?" Sara felt unaccountably annoyed at this discovery.

"Yes and no. It's worth seeing how quick-witted you are when having to complete a task, when there are more efficient means of completing it," Barlay explained. "Just because we have legs and feet, it doesn't mean we are limited to using just them. Our dragons are extensions of ourselves, after all. Think of them as being extensions of those legs and feet, and even your eyes, if you think about it."

Barlay's dragon, now much enlarged from when Sara had seen him less than an hour earlier, landed and then shrank to the size of a large pony, at which point the Dragonguard leader climbed aboard. Once he was firmly settled, the dragon slowly enlarged himself until he was what Sara to be considered a "normal" size for one of the great beasts.

"Is Aya coming, too?" Sara wanted to know.

"Aya? No, she has other things she must do today," Barlay told her. "This is a journey for just the two of us and our dragons. We should return late this evening, Aya unless something urgent comes up while we are visiting the new Aerie."

"Yes, my lord," Aya replied, rendering a loose salute that the elder Dragonguard returned with good humor. "I'll let Gymon know."

"You do that," he said. "So, Sara, are you and your dragon ready? Snow doesn't know why we've waited this long to leave. He wants to fly."

Not waiting for an answer, man and dragon leaped into the air with a yell and a roar of anticipation. Sara followed as quickly as she was able, startled by the suddenness of their departure.

They vaulted into the air, wings flapping mightily in an attempt to catch up with the fast-disappearing Barlay. Sara was taken aback by the fact that she remained firmly seated on the dragon's shoulders when what little she knew of physics told her she should be holding on for dear life. Another piece of the mystery of Dreaming dragons, she supposed.

Barlay and Snow were dwindling into the distance, and Sara put all the energy she could into working to catch up to the two more experienced flyers. It was difficult to focus on Barlay and his dragon, for one, because the stark white hide blended so well with the light blue sky, and two, the scenery below her was breathtaking and kept trying to grab her attention.

When she finally managed to pull alongside the other dragon and his rider, he waved at her, a thick piece of something in his hand, his jaw working hard as he chewed on whatever it was. Then she realized what he was telling her.

Reaching into the small carry sack tethered to her waist, Sara pulled a thick piece of dried meat out and tore a chunk from it, chewing for all she was worth as she worked enough saliva into her mouth to be able to swallow the thing without choking on it. She was surprised to discover that some kind of dried fruit had also been pounded into it, so that gave it a subtle tart sweetness while at the same time, enhancing the savory taste of the well-seasoned meat.

The sudden influx of food helped to reenergize Sara, and she kept chewing at the large piece of meat until she was able to shove the much-reduced remains into her mouth and swallow it down. When she looked at him again, she saw that Barlay was smiling at her.

"Another lesson, child," he told her. "After putting out so much energy, be sure to eat. Never forget to bring additional food with you, or you may regret it terribly."

"I see that my lord," Sara said, trying to put an enthusiasm she did not feel into her tone. "Thank you for the object lesson."

"I know you probably would have liked some forewarning, child, but I've found that it's better to teach this lesson the hard way. Much more difficult to forget it later on, eh?" Barlay explained. "Be happy you don't need to find a way to feed a beast that size. I don't believe you'd find enough meat to manage that, at least, not for long, anyway."

"We certainly eat enough to make up for it," she said, voice raised to be heard over the whispering wind through which they now glided.

"Yes, but overall, you eat much less than a carnivore of equal size would eat over the course of a week," he responded. "Anyhow, this is not science, this is magic, and magic has entirely different rules, as you may know."

"I don't know much about magic, so I'll take your word for it. The only thing I know is that I have a dragon now, for whatever reason, and I can't imagine not having her now."

"That's how it works, Sara. I believe that dragons are just another part of ourselves that cannot be contained inside of us, and when we encounter someone with a similar disposition, that dragon emerges into the light."

"You'd think more people would become Dragonguard," Sara objected. "Isn't everyone like that?"

"I did not express myself well, I suppose," Barlay said. "What I meant to say is that some people have *so much* of themselves trapped inside, that it takes the touch of one who has Dreamed to bring out their own dragon. Their own expanded self."

Sara thought about that as she flew, absently munching on a sweet bean paste-stuffed steamed bun. She had never had one before she had joined the Aerie, but had decided they were a favorite food almost from her first bite of one on the day she arrived and was offered one from a tray of various kinds of steamed buns. Mireya, the middle-aged Dragonguard who ran the Aerie's kitchens and the vast dining hall, had thought to add a few of them to Sara's traveling-food package, knowing that having snacks the Dragonguards enjoyed available would make each rider more inclined to keep their energy up.

Barlay kept talking through most of their flight to the new Aerie. Sara made noises of interest or assent, but for the most part, kept her mouth shut, unless an actual verbal response was required. It was an ingrained habit from her childhood education in the village school. Master Ebelard was strict about keeping silent and paying attention, and Sara had ever been an obedient student in his classroom.

Barlay waxed poetic about his life with his dragon, and how he had come to Dream him, when he was only five years old, having been born in an Aerie several hundred leagues away. Sara wondered what it would be like to have your dragon from the time you were a young child before you had learned whatever it was you needed to know by the time you were an adult. How did that color Barlay's relationship with his dragon and his outlook on life?

Even though the man was, according to Aya, in his 80s, he seemed much younger to Sara. In many ways, he was still that five-year-old boy. Would she be sixteen-year-old Sara for the rest of her life? She ruminated on this in silence.

"Hoy, Sara!" Barlay called to her, pointing down at a rocky mountainside. "Look there!"

Looking down, Sara could see activity below her, with both dragons and humans bustling here and there on the steep slope. She looked back at Barlay.

"Welcome to Granel Aerie!" he announced with his customary smile. "It should be up and running within the fortnight, I believe. We've already put out the call for transfers among the Dragonguard."

"Transfers? So Dragonguard will move from one Aerie to another? Is it that simple?"

"Technically, yes, but when you have Dragonguard who have ties in a certain area, they are more reluctant to make such a move. Usually, it's unattached single Dragonguard who are adventurous enough to do so," he told her. Then he eyed her shrewdly. "What about you? Would you be interested in making such a move? Young people such as yourself are best in a new Aerie, in my experience."

"I've barely settled into my quarters at the Aerie now," she protested.

"Yes, you have, but then, you haven't set roots in the stone there, either. You can settle into the new Aerie here," Barlay told her as the dragons backwinged into a landing on a bare slab of sun-warmed rock. "I'd like you to make this move. I think you'd be of benefit to Granel."

"Of benefit? Howso?" Sara wanted to know. "I'm just one person, and I'm sure others with more seniority would be better suited for this."

"Aya tells me that you know something of smithing, and we don't have one currently able to move shop here. There are no other journeymen with enough training, child."

So that's what was going on. The new Aerie needed personnel, and Sara, it seemed, fit the bill to fill one vacant position.

"That can't be true," she protested. "I'm not the only smith out there!"

"True, there might be others out there, but they are not what Granel needs now."

Sara looked hard at the old man. She saw only sincerity in his eyes, not deceit.

"Has the smithy been set up yet, or does that need to happen as well?" she asked with a sigh of resignation. Barlay smiled again.

"Hansen, our own blacksmith, framed out the bare basics of a permanent smithy for Granel, but it needs the polishing that only a full-time smith can give it. That is what I am asking you to do here."

What would Pharis think if she knew that her sister, who had been a competent though indifferent journeyman smith, was the blacksmith in a Dragonguard Aerie? Would it be wise to share that information with her sister, the next time they saw one another?

"Would this be a permanent position?" she asked Barlay. "Or would I be a placeholder smith?"

"Well, yes, it would be permanent, Sara, but I would not be asking you to consider it if it was not vitally important to have you here," he explained. "Are you worried that some might not take you seriously here?"

That question startled her.

"Does that happen?" she blurted. Everything she had experienced so far in her short time as a Dragonguard seemed to deny that possibility.

"Here? No. I thought that perhaps you were from a country such as our Aya came from before she joined our number," Barlay explained, looking at least as startled as Sara felt. "She said you had considerable skill as a blacksmith, but I did not know much more than that."

When had the Dragonguard had the time to judge her skill at smithing, and then she remembered the filigree work she had shown Aya while she was recovering from her Dreaming. Aya had not demonstrated that she was at all impressed by Sara's work, but it was now clear that she had indeed been impressed.

"It's possible, I suppose," she replied. "Could you show me the smithy as it is now, and I'll see what can be done with it."

"I couldn't ask for more," Barlay said, his satisfaction plain on his broad face. "Let's get something to eat from their canteen before we start our journey, shall we?"

After a dinner of thick meat stew that seemed heavier on meat and less so on vegetables, and fresh hot bread, Barlay began the tour. Sara could tell that the Dragonguard had spent a lot of time here, as it seemed he knew the place like the back of his lined and wrinkled hand. As he passed, some of the residents would smile and wave, which he would return in kind.

"As a founding newcomer," he told her as they walked, "you'd have your choice of quarters here. Assignment of quarters is related to one's length of residence, and you'd be right there at the start, for all intents and purposes."

"Surely the best quarters have already been claimed!" Sara responded to the intriguing suggestion.

"Not necessarily, child," Barlay said. "As the blacksmith, you'd not only have founder's status but personal status with not only this Aerie but all the others."

"I'm not much for status," Sara told him. "It doesn't mean much to me."

"That's fine, Sara," he replied. "I just wanted to let you know what the position here would mean for you."

They walked a bit more, Sara silent as Barlay pointed out this feature and that feature. He stopped when they reached a cave opening that faced out across the broad valley below, the sun already having started its descent toward the horizon beyond. She had not realized the day was so far along.

"Take a look at this view! What do you think," he asked her, gesturing broadly with one arm. "Isn't it lovely?"

Sara took the time to look and was awed by what she saw. There was a long river below that wended its way through a thinly-treed forested area before being interrupted by a torrential waterfall and then continuing on its way. She could see villages scattered here and there in the valley, with outlying farms appearing to bulge with vast fields. Sara wondered how long ago the first settlement had been founded there.

"Yes, it is pretty," she replied. "Very pretty."

"Wouldn't you like to live here and see such beauty every day?"

"I can fly and do that, I think," she said, surprised to hear a note of tartness in her voice. "I'm sorry, I did not mean that the way it came out."

"No harm was done, Sara," Barlay told her. "I wanted you to know that these quarters have not yet been claimed, and they could be yours, along with this beautiful view, if you decided to help build the Aerie."

"I..."

"Just come with me, and I'll show you around."

Obediently following Barlay into the unclaimed quarters, Sara was instantly taken with their sheer size and quality.

Instead of being something constructed by human hands, these rooms appeared to be of natural origin, although some areas had seen the attention of human intervention. In all, there were three spacious rooms connected.

The second-largest room already contained a large bed with a soft, well-stuffed mattress, a massive chest of drawers, a closet built into the wall, of all things, an overstuffed armchair, and two side tables. Wall sconces sporting tallow candles lit all the rooms with a flickering, welcoming light.

The smallest chamber was unfurnished, but Sara could easily see it being the study she craved. There was a rectangular hole in one wall that was filled with a real glass window, framed with dark-stained wood, allowing natural light to brighten the room's interior.

A raised fireplace occupied an outside wall in the main room. It was large enough to heat all three chambers if it was required.

"These quarters are far too fine for someone like me," she challenged Barlay. "Surely the Aerie's leaders deserve something like this!"

"They have already chosen their quarters, and these were set aside for whoever would be the Aerie's blacksmith. You would not be inconveniencing anyone if you signed on to that position," Barlay assured her. "Your skills are needed here, Sara."

Sara set her jaw and looked at the older man. His expression was sincere, and although it was serious, the hint of a smile remained at the corners of his mouth.

"Aren't there others who could take the position, my lord? I'm a no one. A nobody," she protested. "I don't want to offend anyone!"

"Of a certain, there are, Sara," he allowed. "It is simply that some in the Dragonguard Council have decided that going forward, we need to people the Aeries with younger folk. The Dragonguard needs to embrace change, and the only way that will happen is if we bring in those who are more amenable to new ideas."

Sara was surprised to hear such a thing from an elder, and before she could stop herself, said as much. Shocked by her temerity, she gasped, covering her mouth. Instead of anger, Barlay reacted with his customary laughter.

"I understand your shock, my dear, but I am not what I seem," he explained. "In my day, Sara, I was considered to be a hot-headed young progressive, and I try to remain so. I ruffled more than a few feathers among the Dragonguard elders of that time, and even when I was urged to quiet down, I kept my voice raised up. I believe you are someone who would do the same."

"You should have experienced leaders here, my lord," she protested, determined not to step on anyone's toes. His professed faith in her made Sara feel a little uncomfortable. "I don't know much of anything."

"And there will be, I promise you," Barlay said with a warm smile. "You're being asked to be the blacksmith, not the leader of Granel Aerie."

At least, not yet, she read in his eyes.

"Still—" she began, but Barlay cut her off.

"I've been given the task of finding recruits for this new Aerie, and I'm taking that opportunity to help the Dragonguard grow as it should, and your becoming blacksmith here is part of that opportunity," he replied, putting a warm hand on her shoulder. "The leader of this newest Aerie, Hurin, rider of Tempest, is young compared to other leaders but has been a junior Counselor in his home Aerie for a few years now. His time with the Aerie Council has familiarized him with what is required for an Aerie to run smoothly."

Sara looked around the quarters and sighed. The man was not going to take "no" for an answer, it seemed. As she made her decision, the room began to feel familiar, and no longer something she was only visiting.

"Very well," she told him. "Pending the agreement of Hurin to your suggestion, I accept."

"Excellent!" Barlay exclaimed, clapping a hand on her shoulder and squeezing it. "He has already approved your position here, on the strength of my enthusiastic recommendation. Hurin knows how important you and your talents are to this Aerie. You will not regret your decision."

As if I had the option of saying 'no,' she thought but kept her opinion to herself.

12

It was almost two months later, and the smithy had only just been completed to Sara's satisfaction. From her own experience working in her father's smithy and after discussing it further with Pharis, she had drawn up plans for what she would need, and the members of Granel Aerie had not disappointed her.

The smithy was twice the size of the one her father had created for himself, with ample storage spaces for supplies, as well as finished work. Sara had not realized how much she had taken to heart some of her older sister's complaints and observations as Pharis, who tended to talk to herself at the forge, worked.

Her visit to Pharis for that advice had served the dual function of reassuring her family that she was alive and well, that she was happy, and doing useful work. Her mother, forgetting her earlier anger and resentment, had cried tears of joy upon her arrival, enfolding her in a hug, insisting that she at least stay the night.

Dinner was a feast compared to her family's usual midday fare, and Sara was delighted to taste her mother's food once more. When asked about what she ate at the Aerie, she let them know that it was good, filling food, but did not share particulars. Isleni might have felt insulted.

When the meal was completed, and the three women were sharing a lazy dessert of pastry and hot tea, Sara broached the third reason for her visit. She had worked hard on what she planned to say to Isleni and focused on those words now.

"Mum, I was wondering if you would consider selling wool to the Aerie," Sara blurted. "The current supplier is retiring and no longer wants the position."

Isleni sat up, startled at the unexpected suggestion.

"Doesn't the Aerie manufacture their own yarns and threads," Pharis asked.

"With so many people to support, having to support livestock as well can be difficult," Sara explained. "Yes, we do what we can to supply food on our own, but we also buy from non-Dragonguard as well. We want to help support our communities, and if you were willing to accept the contract, the Elders would be very grateful to you. I know the amount of money they're prepared to offer is not insignificant. You would live quite comfortably on the profits of such a venture."

"I couldn't do all of that on my own," Isleni protested. "I'm only one woman, after all."

"As to that, Mum, there is something else." Isleni stared at her daughter, one eyebrow raised as she waited for further explanation.

"Yes?"

"I've discussed this with Barlay, the Elder at my old Aerie, so he agreed to let me discuss it with you. I only ask that you keep it to yourselves, as it is not common knowledge outside the Aerie."

"You see, dragons are *Dreamed* by the human who ends up with theirs. That's how I got my own," she explained to the rapt attention of her sister and mother. "That can happen at any age, but the Dragonguard prefer that children younger than sixteen not chance a Dreaming of their own."

"Because of that from the time a child has just begun to walk until the age of sixteen, they are sent out into the world to learn about the outside world and perhaps learn a trade of their own during that time. There is no sense in keeping them cloistered and only in the company of other Dragonguard. Also, the child may decide they don't yet wish to return to the Aerie if they decide to return at all, so this gives them that opportunity."

"So what are you suggesting, Sara? I'm not in any position to foster infants and toddlers," Isleni replied when her daughter paused long enough for the woman to get a word in edgewise.

"No, not toddlers or anything like that, Mum," Sara reassured Isleni. "I'm thinking children of the age of ten and upward if that's suitable for you. Old enough to need less one-on-one attention, but young enough to be willing to learn. Think of them as apprentices, I suppose."

"How am I supposed to feed all of those empty stomachs? It's enough to feed myself, your sister, and the new hired man, Enulf."

"Of course the Aerie would see you well stocked with whatever you'd need for food, Mum," Sara assured Isleni as firmly as she was able. "The Aerie pays their own way."

"How many of these apprentices could I expect to foster at a time?"

"Only as many as you were comfortable with fostering, Mum," Sara was quick to add. "No one wants to overburden you!"

Sara could see her mother turning the suggestion over and over in her mind. Isleni, never one to jump into anything, would be examining the idea from every possible angle she could discover. After a time that the sisters spent sipping more tea and having a quiet conversation among themselves, Isleni heaved a sigh and cleared her throat.

"On its face, it sounds like it might be a good thing," she said. "I'll sleep on it, and I'll let you know my decision in the morning."

"Thank you, Mum. It's all I can ask of you."

"It seems I may become even more connected with the Dragonguard than I expected," she said with an amused grimace. At least it was better than a frown, Sara supposed. "Dragonguard younglings taking up space and making noise around here."

"If you think it would be a problem, Mum," Sara began.

"If I was against it, you'd know that now, and I would not make you wait on my decision, girl," Isleni said to her daughter. "You be patient with me, and I'll let you know in the morning, noon at the latest."

"Yes, Mum. Thank you so very much for even considering it."

"Mmhmm."

When bedtime came, the sisters once again shared a bed, but instead of sleeping, spent the entire night talking about everything that came into their heads. Sara vowed to herself that she would never stay away so long again. She found it refreshing to spend time with her sister and mother.

Sara's dragon had shrunk down to the size of a sparrow and was nesting atop a high shelf where there would be little chance of either Pharis or Isleni touching her. She had been the subject of intense curiosity upon their unexpected arrival, causing Pharis to squeal like a little girl when Sara demonstrated how the dragon could change size in the blink of an eye.

When Pharis inevitably asked how the dragon had come to be hers, Sara was evasive. The elders had been insistent that she keep that secret, and after consulting Barlay, she complied with that injunction. Blurring the truth a little bit, as she could never outright lie to anyone, Sara explained that with certain people, a dragon would come to them when the time was right.

It was a kind of truth, but not *exactly* the truth. It was the truth as it should be.

She did not share that the dragon and she were one and the same. That was not common knowledge, as the Dragonguard knew that some might want to use that knowledge for nefarious purposes. While she knew that Pharis would never share that kind of information on purpose, Sara felt it was better to keep her ignorant of such this. It bothered her to know she was keeping secrets from her family, but something told her it was the best decision she could make.

SARA'S FIRE

The next morning, as she prepared to leave for the Aerie once more, Isleni pressed a small package on Sara, insisting she take it with her. Hugs and tears were exchanged between mother, daughters, and sisters, and then Sara was on her way back to the Aerie.

An hour of flying later and Sara began to feel hungry. She dug into her waist bag for a piece of dried meat and found her mother's package there. Bits of reddish-brown meat dust were scattered across its surface, as the package had been shoved in with her supply of jerky.

After choosing a suitable piece of meat, Sara pulled out the package and opening it, discovered a pair of snowy-white linen handkerchiefs, embroidered with what could only be the delicate silk thread for which her mother had bartered. Sara's heart caught in her throat as she saw the image of her dragon's head immortalized on the corner of each square of cloth.

Sudden tears of happiness were wicked away from her cheeks with this sign of her mother's quiet blessing of her new life.

13

Inspecting the now-completed smithy, Sara nodded her satisfaction. The construction supervisor's face blossomed with a happy smile. Working with the young woman over the past fortnight had been a lesson in how to do things right the first time. Young she may have been, but it had become apparent to the man that this young woman knew her craft and would settle for nothing but the best.

He found that he respected that attitude and did not resent Sara's demands in that area.

"Thank you for all your hard work, Layen," she praised the man sincerely, taking a pair of long-handled tongs off the wall to check the bolt that bound the two pieces of steel. She placed a single drop of lubricating oil on the mechanism to ease its movement. "I know I'm not an easy person to work with, and your patience with me is appreciated."

"You were no bother, Sara," he assured her, watching as she dawbed a bit of oil on the bolt and then opened and closed the tool's jaws to help spread the lubricant. Her knowledge of her craft never failed to impress him. "Compared to our esteemed Kitchen Master, Dennel, you were a breeze!"

Dennel was the solidly built, gray-bearded man who oversaw the vast kitchens and dining hall. A former Kitchen-Second, he had exacting standards he had learned from his previous Kitchen Master and knew what he needed for his kitchens and dining hall to run as they should. It was easy to underestimate the man at first glance, but it was not long before one realized he was much wiser and athletic than he appeared.

Sara made herself scarce the day Dennel oversaw the gutting and rebuilding of the roasting kitchen. She flew to the ocean's edge and spent the day collecting pretty shells and swimming in the warm salt water. The dragon entertained herself by diving into the deeper parts of the water and surfacing again with live giant clams and otherwise hard-to-obtain sea creatures that would be delicious, once prepared by a knowledgeable chef.

Not having to breathe, the beast was able to search out the most elusive and tasty shellfish available. The sizeable moist bundle Sara brought back with her to the Aerie caused much curiosity and discussion when she returned, as she landed right outside the Kitchen Master's office.

Dennel accepted Sara's unexpected gift when she returned just after sunset, leaving her with a tasty slab of bloody-rare roast beef and an aromatic heap of steamed and spiced river grains, accompanied by a mug full of the thick dark beer he knew she liked.

There was a day-long festival of seafood that began the following morning. Sara discovered tureens of steaming hot clam chowder and ate that at each meal. Dennel himself placed a cloth-covered platter of freshly baked bread alongside her soup plate.

Dennel showed the Dragonguard why building a kitchen, *his kitchen*, right the first time was essential the day after the kitchens were finished. After offering only simple fare for breakfast and dinner presented the Aerie with a celebratory supper feast that including whole roast oxen, several wildfowls, bread both savory and sweet, intricately confected desserts, and more.

Dennel was not one to socialize with the rest of the Aerie, so Sara was surprised when the man sat down to share a meal with her. He stared at her wordlessly, pulling his fingers through his thick beard as though pulling his thoughts together before saying anything.

His hall staff was kept busy running back and forth, keeping drinks filled and platters piled high with fresh offerings from the kitchen. The man spoke little as they dined, which Sara found refreshing. She felt no need to fill things in with conversation when the food was something special to be savored.

"Welcome to the Aerie," Dennel blurted out before putting a fork laden with plump, sweet peas into his mouth. Sara noted that he took a long time chewing each bite of his food, savoring every last bit of it before swallowing it down with a sip of fresh water.

"Thank you, Kitchen Master," she replied. "It is always a pleasure to enjoy your meals."

"Please, call me Dennel," he insisted with a tight smile. Sara had never seen the man smile before, so this must be something special for him. "I'm pleased we've gotten a blacksmith for the Aerie. I imagine you'll be forging all manner of tools and the like."

"I'm sure I will be, but I've always preferred to make dainty little things, like my earrings," she poked gently at the silver and pearl earrings that dangled from her ears. Interest coloring his expression, Dennel leaned forward to take a closer look at the shiny earbobs.

"You made those? They're lovely," he exclaimed, once he sat back in his seat. "You did all that work yourself? Who taught you?"

"My father was a blacksmith, but sometimes, folk would come to him looking for something pretty for themselves or a loved one," she replied. "He was usually tied up with larger things, so he gave those jobs to me."

"It seems you were more than a capable student, then," was Dennel's response with a hint of a chuckle. "If only some of my apprentices were so attentive and accomplished in their lessons."

They fell back into silence and continued their meal. Knowing that the man had no dragon of his own, she was surprised he could eat as much as he did without gaining weight. Of course, as busy as he was, cooking, supervising his staff, and all, the food he consumed never had a chance of going to fat.

"My mother was a Dragonguard, my father the son of a pair of Dragonguards. I had the option of living outside the Aerie, but the Dragonguard was all I knew growing up and are my family now," he told her. "The Kitchen Master at my birth-Aerie encouraged the development of my culinary skills, and now, here I am. I'm pleased that you're enjoying my humble fare."

Sara laughed.

"Humble? Hardly. It is absolutely wonderful!"

The man blushed with pleasure at her amused expression and praise. After finishing his own meal, he had returned to whatever it was he had been doing before coming to eat with her.

Once Sara had eaten her fill and sat back, hands resting on her distended belly, Dennel had been almost shy as he asked her to consider the crafting of a particular ring for a special friend. As he began to describe what he wanted, she saw his eyes soften a bit and knew romantic thoughts when she saw them.

Sara listened to Layen's thoughts on what he had in mind, making suggestions along the way. Once they came to an understanding of what it was that he wanted, Sara shook hands on the bargain.

Now that the smithy was completed, she would be able to fulfill that request.

"Speaking of Dennel," she said, "Go and tell him that you've finished the smithy and that I'm delighted with the results. I think he has something special set aside for you and your crew."

Layen went to his crew, who waited just out of earshot, and must have told them everything, as Sara watched as some of them made exaggerated expressions of relief. A moment later, they all began to move downhill toward the dining hall, grinning and chatting as they went.

"No excuse now," Sara said aloud. "Time to start work!"

Unlocking a particular cabinet, she pulled a small ingot of silver from a shelf and turned it around in her hands, checking it for any apparent impurities. Finding none, she put it into what looked like a small, long-handled saucepan.

"Hey, you, come here," she called to her dragon, who had been sunning herself on the roof. "We've got work to do."

The dragon flitted down and perched on the smithy's wide hearth, folding her tiny wings and cocking her head to one side as she watched Sara, who locked the pot's handle in a fixed clamp and then stepped back.

Opening her mouth, the dragon began to play a continuous jet of fire over the pot's exterior, until it glowed a dull red. Sara stepped forward again, looked down into the smelting pot and gave a satisfied smile.

Wearing a heavy, lined glove as a gauntlet to protect her tender flesh from the pot handle's extreme heat, Sara poured the now-liquid silver into a waiting clay mold. The dragon's part complete for now, the creature gave a happy chirp and went back to her basking spot on the clay-shingled roof.

Once the silver cooled to the point that it was stable enough to more or less keep its shape, Sara broke it free from the clay mold. Sliding it onto a rod of the right size, she began the intricate work of etching a pattern on its exterior. Every few minutes, she called the dragon back to warm the silver enough for her to continue working with it.

Several hours later, the ring was complete, encrusted with alternating fragments of carefully matched amethyst and emerald down the center, otherwise featureless silver borders etched with a pattern of leafy vines, then the whole thing polished to the point where it almost shone with a light of its own. Even Sara considered it to be a masterpiece, and she was her own worst critic.

"She is like having your own little ember at hand, isn't she?" said a familiar voice from behind Sara. She jumped from her seat and spun to see Aya in the doorway.

"How long have you been standing there?"

"Long enough to see how useful she is to you," Aya told her. "I'm impressed. I'm surprised you even need a regular forge when she is there to help."

"It's wonderful to see you again, Aya," Sara enthused, grinning as she enfolded her friend in a massive hug. "Where have you been? I haven't seen you since the day I came here."

"I've been doing Barlay's bidding, of course, looking for new recruits for the Aerie. I don't think I've had a full night's sleep in at least a week!"

"He is a hard man to ignore, isn't he?"

"I gave up trying to tell him "no" ages ago," Aya replied. "It's useless to even think you can do it."

Sara snorted and then realized something.

"You knew I was going to stay here that morning, didn't you?"

Aya managed to look embarrassed. Then she laughed.

"Well, knowing Barlay, I knew it was a foregone conclusion that you would not be coming back, so I made sure all of your things were packed up and delivered after a suitable period of time elapsed," Aya admitted. "I hope you are not mad at me."

"No, I'm not mad, Aya. I would not have believed you if you'd told me this would happen," she told her friend. "Hey, I've got something to deliver to Dennel, if you'd like to join me for supper."

"Supper? I'm famished!"

"When aren't you?"

Both young women began to laugh at this truth. A Dragonguard was always hungry and could eat large quantities of high-calorie foods and never gain an ounce.

"May I see the ring," Aya asked. "I've seen some of your fine work, but never something this detailed."

Sara handed the ring over to her friend, who received the jeweled circle with a kind of reverence. Aya peered at the scrollwork on the edges of the metal and looked up at Sara, eyes wide.

"How can you do such tiny work? The detail is amazing!"

"My father indulged my creativity and encouraged me to practice working with the finer metals. He said that having one daughter working the heavy smithing, he could afford to let me create what he called *frippery*. Making horseshoes and fixing plow blades is important work, but it's not what I want to do *all* the time," she snorted, taking the ring back and giving it another polish to remove any fingerprints. "I made a bit of my own money doing custom work when it came my way."

Sara then wrapped the ring in a piece of soft white silk cloth and then tucked that bundle into a small, delicately stained hinged wooden box, which closed with an elegant silver hasp mechanism. She was very proud of the box, and when others had seen her work, they queued up to order their own.

Upon being presented with the delicately crafted ring, Dennel was so delighted with Sara's work that, after giving her a purse holding his generous payment for her services, he brought out a kind of sweet nut cake that he knew Sara enjoyed when she could get it.

"Someone told me you'd had this at your old Aerie, and liked it. I hope this is at least as good as what you remember from your old home," he told her, blushing with embarrassment.

"I'm sure it is at least as good, if not better," Sara exclaimed, the dessert's sweetness going beyond tastebuds and teasing her sense of smell. "I'm sure I'll enjoy it, Dennel."

The man blushed even more at Sara's compliments, and then excused himself to return to the relative safety of his kitchens.

As intricate as Sara's silver creation had been, the dessert was made of many layers of paper-thin pastry dough filled with rich, tasty nutmeats that had been ground into a savory filling, then baked until it was a delicate golden-brown.

The hot pastry was then slathered with honey thinned only by warming it slightly, for it to permeate the entire confection before it cooled and thickened again. You only ate this pastry with your fingers if you were not bothered by having to lick them clean afterward.

Being the kind of person she was, Sara shared her treat with her newly-returned friend. Her pristine fork remained on the table beside her dessert plate. Something like this was eaten with fingers. Forks were just silly.

14

The candle on the small table at which they sat flickered and fluttered as it worked against a slight breeze to stay alight. Sara found it to be almost hypnotic and soothing. The flame was something familiar, a friend upon which she could depend when necessary. With her flame-colored dragon, she had found the same kind of familiarity and dependability. It seemed fitting.

A short time after disappearing into his kitchens, Dennel returned, bringing with him a small bottle of his favorite liqueur to their table and poured two aperitif glasses with the precious fluid before leaving Sara and Aya alone. She did not think to ask what it was but knew the slightly-built man would not risk offending her.

Raising the narrow glass to her eyes, she could see the light of the fire that burned on one wall through the thick, sweet amber alcohol. Taking a sip, she put the glass down beside her plate, considering the taste. The taste of the stuff reminded her of honey, though would never have thought to present it in a fermented form.

"What is this?" Sara asked her friend, pointing at the liqueur. "Do you know what it is? It's delicious!"

"You've never had mead before?" Aya asked her, incredulous. "I'm surprised. It's made of honey. There is a brewer in one of the other Aeries who makes a few barrels of it each year, and he is sweet on me, so he gives me a bottle of it when I visit."

"Fermented honey? That explains the taste, I suppose. My family doesn't make a habit of drinking," Sara explained. "I only had my first drink of alcohol a few weeks ago, and that was at the first Aerie I ever saw. Smallbeer, they said it was. I had never heard of that before, so when I asked what that meant, the new Aerie brewer, Arnet, explained it to me."

Small beer was the standard beverage that was provided at afternoon and evening meals in Aerie dining halls. It contained very little alcohol but contributed a charming accent to most of the meals Sara had eaten since joining their number. Sara preferred to drink it with a small amount of tart fruit juice added to her mug.

"Arnet is very good at brewing," Aya replied. "He trained under some of the most accomplished brewmasters in the Aeries. This Aerie is very lucky that he has established herself here."

"I'm learning that there is a lot more out here in the world than I realized while I was in my home village, certainly," Sara said to her friend. "Alcohol was not a common thing in our home, as Mum thinks poorly of it. I've been trying new things when I can since I *Dreamed* my dragon, though. Small beers were something I had never considered until now."

"That must have been a surprise to you, then," Aya replied. "I've been drinking small beers since I was a child. It was the only way to be sure we had something safe to drink, as we drank from the same channel that ran through our fields, and turning that water into beer seemed to make the water safe, although I have no idea why that would be. Have you had stronger beers, since?"

"A few," Sara said. "I prefer the dark, thick beers to the yellow ones, though. The yellow ones often taste too sharp to me."

"To each their own, I suppose," Aya smiled, and then pointed at her own glass, which was only half-full now. "So far, I like all the beers I've had. I must say, though, if I could have more of this stuff, I'd be a happy woman!"

Both young women laughed and smiled. Sara had not realized how much she missed her new friend but knew that was because she had been kept so busy since her arrival in the Aerie. Hard work, she had long ago discovered, cleared the mind of many of one's cares.

"Does she help you out a lot with your work," Aya asked. "I'd think to have her around would be more than a little useful in a pinch, when you're a blacksmith. You don't have to go looking for a handy ember to stoke a new fire."

"My dragon as an ember?" Sara laughed. "Yes, I find her to be a much more reliable heat source than the forge when I'm working on some things."

"I've seen that they can create fire hotter than I've seen anywhere else," Aya said, an odd look darkening her normally happy expression. "A fire that burns things completely away until only a tiny pile of ash remains."

The blonde-haired woman's voice seemed to grow hollow as it trailed off. Then Aya came back to herself, shaking her head as though to clear it of whatever dark thoughts she had entertained in the privacy of her memories.

Sara could tell that this involved something serious but did not pry. If Aya wished to share her meaning, she would when and if the time was right if that time ever arrived.

"I've seen that, too," Sara said with more perkiness than she felt, trying to change the mood to take the shadow from her friend's expression. "I went through a few pieces of equipment before I learned to limit how hot a fire I – she – was creating. If regular blacksmiths had access to dragons, they'd never again need to stoke a fire."

"Better they keep doing things the way they are, Sara," Aya cautioned, the hint of a smile teasing the corners of her mouth. "Too many dragons near regular humans could be a disaster. You keep your little portable ember to yourself. Don't even show what she can do to your family. Allow their embers to be made of wood and coal. Dragon-made embers need to stay with Dragonguard."

"Pharis would be disappointed I'm sure, but–"

Sara had been picking up crumbs from the serving platter with a moistened fingertip as Aya spoke, licking them away, then stopped, index finger hovering half an inch from the dish. Her eyes went wide, mouth dropping open with sudden realization. It had been so undeniable, so natural, that she had missed it!

A thrum filled her body, a solid wash of searing heat and icy cold that etched itself into her bones, bringing back the memories of her Dreaming. The white-hot iron of her physical self was quenched and strengthened into the shining steel of truth.

At the same time, a roar from outside the dining hall was echoed by the other dragons within and without the vast chamber. The thrum left her body tingling and shaking with a feeling of delayed recognition.

"Ember!" she shouted at the top of her lungs, forgetting that she was not alone. "Ember!"

The dragons roared again, this time with increasing urgency, and Sara's own dragon, now the size of a tiny hummingbird, darted into the room, hovering over Sara's head, wings beating madly. The creature seemed to glow like a little phoenix afire, a shooting star in miniature, but one that was not reduced to ashes as it burned.

"Your name is Ember!" she shouted, recognizing that it had always been so, and instead of being shocked at Sara's unexpected outburst, the other Dragonguard in the room cheered their approval.

"Ember," she murmured, and the newly-named dragon landed on her shoulder, rubbing her tiny head against Sara's flushed cheek. Sara's dragon-self continued to glow with her own internal flame, but that heat did not burn her human-self. Sara knew with an unshakable certainty that her dragon's heat and flames would be harmless to her and her alone. She could stand in the middle of a blast of Ember's hottest fire and remain unscathed.

"Hello, Ember."

There was a great rush of wind and noise as what seemed to be all of the Aerie's dragons flew into the dining hall, diving and swooping around Sara and Ember, bugling their joy. The fast-moving riot of color was dizzying to look at, forcing Sara to look away.

Ember left her comfortable perch on Sara's shoulder and joined in the expression of aerial congratulations. Sara rose and trailed along behind her joyous beast, the new-named dragon following the other dragons as removed themselves to the open sky, where they enlarged to their customary proportions and continued their aerial ballet, Ember a fiery glow in their midst, her brilliance rivaling the golden-yellow fire of the setting sun.

The humans left behind in the hall stood and applauded, bestowing warm congratulations on Sara, who, having named her dragon, was now, officially, one of their number.

Dennel, who had seemingly been out of eye and earshot only a moment earlier, presented a honey and nut pastry to Sara, cleverly nested in an artful crumple of waxed paper. The smile he bestowed upon her was at least as warm and welcoming as the dragons'.

"I've been making one of these every day since I met you, young lady, anticipating this most happy event," he told her, leaning down to whisper in her ear. "I know it's one of your favorites, after all!"

He grinned conspiratorially at Aya, who joined the man in delighted laughter. Sara looked from one to the other and sighed with amused resignation. Ember, hovering over Sara's head, chittered with draconic laughter.

"Why am I not at all surprised?" Sara asked, a wry expression on her face. She slipped one arm around Dennel's broad shoulders and gave him a squeeze. "Okay, then, who wants a bite?"

"I thank you, dear girl, but this is all yours!" he told her with a broad grin. "Enjoy it all. You'll need it."

15

S ara was exhausted, and not a little drunk, after a long day and evening filled with feasting, drinking, celebration, congratulations and small gifts pressed upon her by the other Dragonguard of the Aerie.

It seemed she had taken a turn around the Aerie's entertainment hall at least once with almost every member of her small community, at least as far as her aching calf muscles were concerned. Although alcohol could initially dull the senses, there would still be the piper to pay once its relaxing effects wore off. She was not drunk enough to forget that truth.

Arnet and Aya had escorted Sara to her quarters, and gotten her tucked snug into bed. She was muzzily aware that there had been a quiet argument over who would stay the night with her.

When she left the comfortable warmth of her bed the next morning, she saw that both had indeed remained. Aya had taken one of the two overstuffed armchairs as a bed, her long, muscular legs stretched across an ottoman, while Arnet was stretched out across the couch, his solid frame covered in the colorful woolen blanket one of the Dragonguard (*who had that been?*) had bestowed upon Sara the previous evening.

Sara filled her iron kettle with water and set it to boil over the hearth fire, then went about taking out a thick hard block of pressed dried tea and some sweet tea biscuits from a cupboard. Her friends would need something to break their fast, once they awakened.

After a moment's thought, she returned the dainty handpainted teacups she had first chosen to their high shelf and replaced them with the large, rough brown stoneware mugs that would hold several times as much tea in one pour. Another moment's thought and she doubled the amount of rolled, dry tea leaves in her waiting teapot. Strong cups of the stimulating beverage would surely be welcomed by both of her friends.

Sara put a fresh pot of water over the fire to boil, as she knew they would not be satisfied with a single cup of tea. Even she averaged two large cups of tea a day when she could manage it.

The tea had steeped from having a slight pinkish color to a very dark cast by the time Arnet opened his eyes. Aya was sitting across from him in the relative darkness of the chamber, sipping from her own mug.

She looked at the iron teapot atop its trivet on the sitting room table, and one of two empty mugs and Arnet nodded, his sleepy expression grateful. Aya smiled and obliged him.

Using a thick towel to protect her fingers from the hot metal of the pot's handle, Aya poured out the steaming tea and passed it over to Arnet, who leaned forward, grabbed a few largish lumps of sweet crystals from their dainty metal bowl , and plopped them into the steaming depths of his mug beside the trivet, gently stirring the contents of the mug with the slender off-white ceramic spoon Aya offered him.

"Thanks," he whispered and took a careful sip. Aya was rewarded with the man's smile of pleasure. "Wonderful!"

"Have some biscuits, please," Aya picked up the platter of sweet biscuits and offered them to Arnet. He picked out two that were topped with much smaller versions of the golden sweet crystals Arnet had put into his tea, and then sat back, teacup in one hand, and one of the two biscuits resting on his knee.

"You know I can hear you, right? Right now, I think I could hear a flea fart in the next room," growled a voice nearby. "I'd like some tea and biscuits, too, if you don't mind."

Sara looked over and saw Aya glaring at her, one eye half-open while the other was still closed, and stifled a giggle. Sentinel was perched on her shoulder, a similar expression on her reptilian face. The dragon hissed, then stretched her wings and settled them neatly down onto her back once more.

"Hungover?" Sara asked her blonde friend a little too brightly. "You're the one who taught me not to mix my alcohols. You should have listened to your own lessons."

The tiny blue dragon on Aya's shoulder gave a low, unhappy growl that was surprisingly loud for such a small creature. Sara was learning very fast that a dragon could make it very difficult to hide one's thoughts and feelings when one was still new to the Dragonguard. Barlay and his dragon, by contrast, were as inscrutable and imperturbable as no one else Sara had ever seen.

"Never you mind that, girl. Give me some of that tea," Aya grumbled, waving her hand vaguely in the air. "And keep it coming!"

Sara giggled and then did as Aya requested. The blonde girl pushed her long hair out of her eyes and twisted it into a rude knot at her neck before she took the food and drink she was offered. Aya made a face and then took a careful sip of the tea, both eyes closed.

She sighed and took another sip. A hint of a smile lifted the corners of her mouth.

"What? You thought it would taste of medicine?" Arnet asked from his corner of the room. "It's tea, for the gods' sake, woman!"

Aya ignored the man's teasing, and even her dragon seemed caught up in the thrill of her first taste of hot tea that morning. For a creature with an immobile set of lips, Sara would have sworn she saw a grin blossom on the scaled mouth.

The dark cloud seemed to lift from Aya's expression as her body assimilated the hot, caffeinated beverage. Another moment, and she took a long drink of the steaming beverage, smiling with satisfaction and sitting back in her chair.

"I love this tea, Sara. I'll have to get some for myself, I think," Aya told her friend. "I can already feel it melting down the ache in my brain!"

An expression of contentment suffused her, and she gave a deep sigh of satisfaction. Rather than nibbling at the biscuit in her hand, she put the entire thing in her mouth, chewed it up, and swallowed it with another drink of the tea. The second cookie soon followed the first, and Sara provided Aya with two more of the sweet treats.

Arnet had only eaten one biscuit so far and had consumed it in two or three bites. He looked down at his second cookie and then glared over at Aya, who eyed the biscuit with an avaricious expression on her face.

"Try to take my biscuit, and we'll come to blows, woman," he told Aya, eyebrow raised. "I'll defend it to the very end!"

Aya snorted.

"As if I'd eat *your* biscuit, Arnet!"

"Oh, come on, you two," Sara broke in, getting up and bringing a heavy ceramic jar to the sitting area table. Looking into the teapot, she saw that it was empty of water, only the mess of soaked, unrolled leaves of tea remaining to decorate its interior. Their rich aroma teased her nose.

Sara poured more hot water into the waiting teapot, watching as the water was stained with the essence still contained in the wet leaves pasted to the bottom of the container. She could refill the pot twice before she needed to consider putting new leaves into it. "I have more biscuits available. Have as many as you like!"

"Leave it to you to ruin my fun," Aya muttered, then softened her tone with a grin. "Let's go and have some breakfast in the dining hall. No sense in decimating Sara's larder if we don't need to do it!"

She realized that Arnet was staring at her and glanced away. She had refilled the pot twice before her guests began to seem restive. The biscuits, however many there had been, had been decimated, and Sara wondered what other treats she might find in her tiny larder to fill their lack.

Then Arnet came to the rescue. Sitting up and gulping down the last bit of tea from his mug, the man stood. He set the empty cup down on the table with exaggerated care.

"That sounds like a wonderful idea, dear Dragonguard," he said to Aya, giving an exaggerated bow to that luminary. "Let us away to Dennel's domain, where we may sample his fine comestibles!"

"Providing he is not half as hungover as we are, Arnet," Aya commented. "I think he put away half a barrel of that liqueur Eyna distilled for the occasion."

Arnet snorted as he recalled the big man waving his empty tankard under the barrel's tap and demanding it be filled. Eyna was known for his strong alcoholic creations.

"If he is hung over, we should bring him some of Sara's wonderful restorative tea," Arnet suggested. "It has certainly helped *me* this morning!"

Both Sara and Aya dissolved in laughter, and they followed Arnet out of Sara's quarters arm-in-arm in giddy anticipation. Their three dragons, now full-sized, flew overhead, great wings booming with each massive downstroke through the crisp morning air.

Epilogue

The kitchens were bustling, everything moving like the well-oiled machine that it was. Food was prepared, plated, and taken out to fill the bellies of the hordes of hungry people in the dining hall. Dirty dishes were hauled back into the kitchens to be washed, dried, and then set out in clean stacks once more to be used by the next set of hungry mouths.

It was a never-ending process that only worked because the man who organized it all knew how each tiny part of that process worked.

That luminary was now taking a few minutes' break and was in his office with the elderly leader of the Aerie. Both were feeling a bit tender in the head after the festivities of the previous evening, so a bit of quiet was welcome.

"Have you heard about what happened in Lordanei," Barlay asked Dennel, who was pouring a mixture of strong coffee and a bit of grain alcohol into a pair of ancient pewter tankards that normally spent their time in his private cabinet. "I've not heard anything first hand, mind you, but the stories I've heard are similar enough that I think they're true."

The Kitchen Master put the two tankards down on the small table beside a pair of heavy ceramic platters and sat with the Aerie's leader. Dennel pursed his lips and absently ran his fingers through the coarse hair on the top of his head. Barlay recognized it as an unconscious expression of emotional discomfort.

Dennel took a deep breath, his expression radiating his concern.

The kitchen and dining hall workers, who passed through their day amongst so very many of the Dragonguard, but who remained almost invisible as they did so, had long been urged to pass along anything interesting they heard to their master. Dennel made a written note of anything that sounded as though it might have some truth to it. Anything of particular concern was passed along to the Aerie's leaders.

"I've heard the rumors, and it's not good, Barlay," Dennel replied, taking a long drink from his tankard. He pointed at a tall pile of paper on the table that was held in place by a bowl half full of small, round, yellow and orange fruits.

"That's just the bits that seemed real," he explained. "If even half of it is true, we're going to have to act. We cannot allow it to continue."

"You get word on just about anything that happens in the world, my friend. Please keep your ears open for anything more, especially if there are specifics offered."

"Of course!"

"I'm sending out some operatives to see what they can find out," Barlay said, smearing a generous helping of soft butter onto a healthy slab of fresh bread. "Aeriefolk, but no one who has Dreamed a dragon. Whoever I send needs to be able to blend in and not cause anything unfortunate while they're spying for me."

He took a big bite of the buttered bread, chewed it up, and then washed it down with a gulp of the mixture in his tankard. Barlay nodded his appreciation of Dennel's "morning after" cure.

"I'll keep my ears open, Barlay and pass along anything else I hear about it," Dennel promised. "Tell you what. I was thinking about sending out some of my stores staff to buy some special supplies. I'll tell them to find out what they can while they're out there."

"Thank you, Dennel," Barlay replied, tossing back what remained of the liquid in his tankard. "I truly appreciate everything you do on behalf of the Aerie."

"My pleasure, Barlay," Dennel said. "You're my family, and I'll do whatever I must to keep my family safe."

"This is going to get worse before it gets good you know," Barlay said. "We've been lucky for a long time, but even luck has to run out every so often."

"Let's try not to take it there, my friend," Dennel told the old man. "We're doing everything we can to keep everyone safe. For now, anyway, I don't think *they* know that we're on to them, and that gives us an advantage."

"Yes, but how long will that ignorance last, Dennel? Well, you tell your people to keep their heads down and not to do anything stupid while they're out there. The world outside is not like the Aerie."

"I only send out people who know that, Barlay. Always. In fact, I recently took in a young man who while dragonless, will be an invaluable asset in our investigation," Dennel commented. "I believe he may have arrived in the Aerie at almost the same time at our esteemed Sara."

"Oh? Who would that be?"

"A young man called Manu," Dennel explained. "It seems he has a gift for remembering things, and that's a gift I think we have a great need for right now."

"Manu? The name is familiar – oh yes. Manu. He was a ward of Isleni Intelo, Sara's mother," Barlay exclaimed, realization in his eyes. "There was a chance he would have Dreamed a dragon, so he was brought to Sara's first Aerie as a preventive measure. When it was shown that he would not have a dragon, he was moved to one of the creches where Aerie children his age reside."

"That's no longer the case my friend," Dennel advised Barlay. "I need to take advantage of his unique gift. When first I heard of him, I was skeptical as to his abilities, so I took a day trip out to the creche to meet him. After only a short conversation, I discovered that he is more than bright enough to be a help to the Dragonguard community. One only has to know how to interact with him in a manner he is able to easily grasp."

"There is a great concern that unreliable individuals might discover his ability and take advantage of him and it," Barlay cautioned as his recollection of the boy solidified in his mind. "I'd hate to see that happen here."

"I suppose that yes, it is a kind of taking advantage, Barlay, but I don't see that we have any alternative, at least for now," Dennel admitted. "I consider the boy to be a gift from the gods, quite frankly. We need someone who can listen in on what is being said out in the world and be able to relate what he hears back to us at the Aerie. Manu can do that for us. His appearance is so unremarkable as to allow him to blend into almost any situation, and that's what I need at a time such as this."

"Indeed, Dennel, but I can't approve this without discussing matters with the boy himself. Will you abide by his wishes and my final decision on the matter?"

"Of course, Barlay," Dennel assured him. "I would not have it any other way. He's currently in the back kitchen cavern, rather industriously peeling tubers, away from the general population of the Aerie."

Barlay snorted at the news.

"Already under your wing, eh, Den?" he noted. "Well, thank you for your foresight in keeping him under wraps. I'm assuming you've kept his identity close to the vest."

The Kitchen Master managed to look offended even while his eyes held a twinkle of amusement. Not for the first time, Barlay was grateful for the man's continuing wisdom.

"I could hardly take the chance of someone recognizing him elsewhere, now could I," the big man noted. "Feel free to go have a chat with him, but make sure he finishes the task to which I've set him tonight. Young Manu seems to feel some level of accomplishment when he completes his tasks."

"You're a hard taskmaster, my friend," Barlay said, smiling at Dennel. "Who'd have thought such an accomplished spymaster would be able to boil water without burning it, much less teach others the same trick?"

Dennel laughed, a deep chortle that came from somewhere down in the vicinity of his big toes.

"Would you have me any other way, old man?" he asked with a broad grin. "Now let me get back to work. I've got to get supper out before I send out the night's messages."

GLOSSARY

Aerie/Dragonhold – Place where Dragonguard and their dragons reside.

Arnet – (Ar'NET) – Dragonguard and Brewmaster of Granel Aerie.

Aya – (Eye'yuh) – Dragonguard at Golden Aerie. The rider of Sentinel. The catalyst of Sara's Dreaming.

Barlay – (Bar'LAY) – Leader of Golden Aerie.

Dennel – (Deh'NEL) – Kitchen Master of Granel Aerie. Beer aficionado. Master of Granel Aerie intelligence network. Son of Darellon.

Eyna – (Ay'nuh) – Master Distiller at Granel Aerie.

Farél – (Fuh'REL) - Blacksmith. Father to Sara and Pharis Intelo. Deceased. Husband of Isleni Intelo, father of Pharis and Sara Intelo.

Garland – (Gahr'land) – Farrier

Isleni – (Iss'leh'nee) - Mother to Sara and Pharis Intelo. Wife of Farél Intelo.

Layen – (Lay'YEN) – Construction supervisor at Granel Aerie.

Mikkel – (My'kel) – Dragonguard at Golden Aerie.

Onari – (Oh'naw'ree) – Traveling entertainer with a very small dark bay stallion that wears silver shoes.

Pharis – (Fair'ISS) - Blacksmith. Daughter of Farél and Isleni Intelo. Sister of Sara.

Randic – (Ran'dik) Itinerant tinker. Teller of tall tales.

Sara Intelo – (Seh'ruh) - Metalsmith. Daughter of Farél and Isleni Intelo.

Don't miss out!

Visit the website below and you can sign up to receive emails whenever Anna Rose publishes a new book. There's no charge and no obligation.

https://books2read.com/r/B-A-MFMF-JYYS

BOOKS 2 READ

Connecting independent readers to independent writers.

About the Author

Anna Rose is the author of the Tales of the Dragonguard (about dragons, of course!) and The Sumaire Web series of vampire novels.

She is currently working on KAL'S HEART, the third story in the Tales of the Dragonguard, that began with AYA'S DRAGON, and continues with SARA'S FIRE. which is now available in both e-book and softcover at Amazon, and in ebook format at iTunes, Barnes & Noble, and other fine merchants.

KAL'S HEART continues the story of the high-flying Dragonguard. Kal, the Aerie-born son of Dragonguard parents, is faced with a mystery that affects not only the whole of the Dragonguard, but his family as well. Together, he and his unusual dragon, Spirit, must use their unique abilities to find out who is causing trouble for the Dragonguard and to his family.

Her newest venture with her stories and novels is turning them into audiobooks for those folks who prefer listening to books, rather than reading them, for whatever reason.

Amongst her other writing, Anna writes vampires who like what they are and aren't looking for a rescue. Her vampires bite, drink and kill. No bottled or bagged blood for these vampires!

The first novel in the series, SIOFRA, was released in late January of 2012. The first novel was followed by FIACH FOLA and then DROCH FOLA. There is also a short story called FEASTA FOLA. Anna is also working on the fourth novel in the Sumaire Web series, COSAN FOLA, which she hopes to have completed by the end of 2018.

She lives in usually sunny Southern California.

Read more at www.sumaire.com.